The Girl from the Sea

Barbara Evans

i

DEDICATION

To all overcomers everywhere.

I am a man upon the land
I am Selkie on the sea
And when I'm far and far frae land
My home it is in Sule Skerry.

CHAPTER 1

By the time he got to the top of the cliffs his leg was aching and he was out of breath. He flung himself down on the grass and stared up at the wide expanse of blue sky and watched through half-closed eyes the slow passage of plump white clouds. As soon as he regained his breath he turned onto his stomach, dragging his sketch book out of his bag, sat up, and studied the landscape around him.

This was only the third time he'd been to the top of the cliff and already he was aware that his leg was stronger and he'd reached the top much quicker. He scrabbled around in his bag and brought out a variety of pencils, flipping through the book till he found a blank page. In front of him was a bunch of harebells, their fine stalks, as fine as a hair, bending in the stiff breeze that blew in from the sea. He studied them carefully then sitting up, began to draw, his delicate pencil lines imitating the fragility of the stems and flowers, although he knew these plants were very tough indeed and withstood the harshest weather.

When he was satisfied with his drawing, he reached for his bag again and brought out a box of watercolour paints, a screw-top jar of water and a few soft paint brushes. He began to wash the drawing with delicate colour. The painting dried quickly, so he closed the book and set his bag on top to stop it blowing away and stood up, shading his eyes and gazing out to sea.

It was then that he saw her. A girl was running across the sand, stopping every now and then to gaze into a rock pool. The wind whipped her hair across her face and tugged at her billowing skirt. She jumped and skipped and then turned cartwheels as if celebrating the joy of movement.

Connor squirmed with envy. He'd never be able to move like that, flinging his arms and legs around with such abandon. But how did she get to the cove? It could only be reached by boat or the dangerous steps cut into the cliff face, and she certainly hadn't passed Connor to climb down the steps, he would have seen her.

He limped over to the head of the steps and stood gazing down at the girl on the beach wondering if she would look up and see him, but at the moment, she was too absorbed in the pools, breaking off every now and then to run madly across the sand twirling around and around as if she was dancing with the wind.

Glancing at his watch, Connor realised he had to make a move. It would take him a while to walk back to the village in time for the mid-day meal. He had another look at his harebell painting and smiled in satisfaction, sliding the book carefully into his bag along with his paints, water jar and brushes.

Travelling down the slope was as uncomfortable as struggling up, different muscles ached, but he was determined to keep going. He wanted his leg to get stronger, he wanted to be able to run, maybe not as fast as the other boys in his class but faster than a limping walk!

He reached the cottage in good time. His mother was putting out home-made bread and ladling steaming soup into bowls.

"Where have you been this morning Connor? I didn't see you in the park when I went to deliver the ironing." Connor's mother took in ironing to supplement their tiny income.

"Oh, just around." He evaded her question. "I found some harebells and made a painting."

"Show me when you've finished your soup."

"Is Dad up yet?" Connor asked as he helped himself to

a hunk of soft brown bread and broke it in two.

"He's up and out. Getting the boat ready for tonight's fishing trip. I've got a pile of ironing to do this afternoon for Mrs Robertson. She wants to collect it at four o'clock so I must get on. Will you stay in this afternoon? You've been out all morning. You shouldn't tire that leg of yours." Connor frowned.

"If I don't use it, it won't get strong and I want it to get strong."

"All the exercising in the world won't make it grow." Her voice was hard and bitter. Connor stared down fixedly at the table, his mouth in a straight line. Then rose abruptly, pushing away his empty soup dish. His mother's hand went to her mouth as if to recapture the words just spoken.

"I'm sorry Connor that came out wrong." He half turned in the doorway.

"No it didn't, you're right, but I'm not giving up."

***

Connor McKenzie had been born with one leg shorter than the other which meant that walking was tiring, and running impossible even though he had a special insole in his shoe to lift his shorter leg. He had a dull ache in his back most of the time which made him very cross and grumpy on occasions.

He was a good-looking boy with light brown hair, the colour of caramel, that formed soft curls like bubbles if it got too long. Most of the time it was too long, he didn't care what he looked like. He had a wide, full-lipped mouth that was always ready to smile, masking the inward ache of loneliness caused by his disability. His eyes, the colour of the ocean in Summer could sometimes blaze with life, but were more often filled with a wistful longing to join in with

3

the other lads at school. But because he couldn't, he spent a lot of his time watching, which resulted in him developing his talent for drawing.

In school, the other youngsters in his class weren't unkind, but they had given up inviting him to join in with them a long time ago, as the games were far too active for Connor and he was too slow, so in the end he just kept refusing, saying he was happy to watch... which wasn't true. He longed to be able to run about like the other boys.

One of the teachers, though, Mr Morrison, took an interest in Connor, and recognising his gift for drawing and painting, encouraged him to take every opportunity to draw and sketch, not just flowers and birds, but people as well. So while the lads in his class were running about and Connor sat on the wall watching, he would get out his sketch book and do lightning quick drawings of the boys and girls in the playground. The youngsters were thrilled to see themselves in Connor's sketch book, and would call out.

"Hey Connor watch this!"

"Try and draw this Connor!" and at the end of playtime, they would crowd around him to see what he'd drawn. But although this was fine and he was pleased that his class mates liked his drawings, it wasn't enough, he wanted to do what they were doing, not just draw it.

So, at weekends when the lads were at football practice he would take off and make himself walk, pushing himself to walk a bit further every time in order to strengthen his leg. He was determined that one day he would run and in spite of what his mother had said he believed he would succeed.

This particular afternoon he decided to walk down to the harbour to watch the fishermen preparing the boats. They would sail out in the evening to reach the fishing grounds just as the fish were rising. Then they would get a good catch.

The men were bustling about making sure everything was clean and tidy, checking the gear that sent out and brought in the nets, and preparing the deck areas. Connor sat on a bollard and began to sketch the men. He could see his father but didn't want to draw attention to himself by calling out or waving. He knew that his father was disappointed in him, as Connor would never work with him on the fishing boats because of his leg.

He decided to complete his sketch, by adding colour, later in the evening. He made notes on the back describing the colours to help him get them right. When he'd finished, he limped down the high-street. The boys were drifting up from the playing fields, flushed and excited from their football training.

"Hi Connor!" they called. "Want to join us in the cafe?" They surrounded him. "We'll buy you a coke. We've got a match next Saturday and Mr Baxter thinks we've got a good chance of beating them." Connor grinned at their excitement and followed them into the tiny cafe. Danny slowed his steps to keep pace with Connor.

"What you been up to then?"

Connor shrugged. "Went for a walk, did some drawing. Nothing very exciting."

Danny grinned. "Show me when the others have gone. I think your drawings are great. I'd love to be able to draw like that." They pushed their way through the doors and joined the rest of the boys all nattering at the same time about the coming match, making quite a din. Connor watched their animated faces longing to get out his sketch book and capture the atmosphere but instead committing it to memory to use later.

When the crowd began to split up and make their way home, Danny walked alongside Connor as 'home' for them was in the same direction.

"Show me your drawings," Danny said. So Connor pulled out his sketch pad from his bag and opened up the last few pages. Danny whistled in appreciation when he saw the sketches of the fishermen on the quay. "D'you know what? I think you could sell these in the shop, if you could make them into a postcard or something. Tourists would love these. 'Scenes by local artist'. Go like hot cakes."

"I'll think about it," Connor replied as they reached his front door. "It's great that you like them."

CHAPTER 2

Danny Stewart was a tall pleasant boy with a thatch of dark, wavy hair and brown eyes that always seemed to sparkle with life. He was very popular with both the boys and girls in his year group. One girl in particular found him irresistible and sought his company on every possible occasion, until Danny succumbed to her charms and she became his girlfriend. Her name was Moira, she had long reddish-brown hair that was very straight and glossy and hazel eyes that noticed everything and jealously protected her relationship with Danny. For this reason, she disliked Connor intensely as Connor was Danny's best friend.

The Sunday afternoon following the football practice, Danny called round to Connor's house, only to find he was out already, but Danny knew where to find him. He set off out of the village taking the steep path to the cliff top. When he reached the top he spied Connor sitting on a rock, sketch book on his knee concentrating so hard he was unaware of Danny arriving and jumped when Danny flung himself down on the grass beside him.

"Good job I wasn't drawing just then!" Connor remarked.

"How's the leg shaping up?" Danny asked plucking a grass stem and chewing the juicy stalk.

"Oh, you know, I think it's getting stronger. I time myself every time I come up here and I am getting quicker but it's taking ages." He sighed. "I don't know that I'll ever be able to run like you and the others."

"Yeah, I know, and I'll never be able to draw and paint like you." Danny groaned and gave an exaggerated sigh. Connor punched him playfully on his shoulder and Danny rolled over in the grass.

"You know it's different! Anyway where's the lovely Moira this afternoon?"

"Gone over to the main island for the day with her

parents. She wanted me to go too." He pulled a face. "Why would I want to do that?... Are you up to walking a bit further?"

"Yep, but, I know what I'd like to do."

"What's that?"

"I'd like to walk down the steps to the beach."

"Whoa, those steps are dangerous for anyone with two good legs, but..." His voice trailed into silence.

"I know." Connor lifted his head and looked steadily at his friend.

"The rail is broken in some places," Danny protested.

"I know," Connor said again. "That's why I need you to help me. I'd love to walk on the sand."

"And then you've got to come back up again!" Danny exclaimed. "Will you have the strength?"

"Don't know till I try." Connor's gaze fell, his fingers tugging distractedly at the tuft of grass at his feet.

Danny sighed. "I don't think this is a good idea."

"You sound just like my mother!" Connor turned resentful eyes on Danny. "If you won't help me I'll do it alone."

"Connor it's dangerous!"

Connor got to his feet and began to limp towards the top of the steps. He didn't look back.

"OK! If you really want to."

Connor looked back, a slow grin spreading across his face, his eyes beginning to dance. He waited by the empty iron basket of the millennium beacon, as Danny walked slowly towards him and the edge of the cliffs where the steps began.

"I'd better go first," Danny said. "Then if you fall you fall into me."

"That's great, then we both go over," chuckled Connor. "I'll hang on to the rail when it's there, and on to you when it's not."

They began to descend the steps. They were rough and

irregular, with bits broken off and some steps crumbling. Danny called out warnings to Connor who followed, gripping the rail tightly. The rail itself was wobbly in places; where it was broken altogether, Danny waited patiently for his friend, and taking his hand made sure he walked on the inside nearest to the cliff face.

Half-way down there was a section where a few steps had partly crumbled into the sea and the rail was missing. So Connor had to navigate these steps clinging onto the cliff wall. Danny watched, his heart in his mouth.

"Have you had enough now?" He asked his friend who looked rather pale. "You've done really well to have got this far!"

Connor took a deep breath and blew out slowly, puffing out his cheeks.

"I think I'll sit for a bit, then I suppose we'd better head back. I'm really glad we did it though. Thanks Dan. I can't wait to get to the beach."

"Well you can't rush it. I'll give you a hand another time and maybe we can get a bit further. Ready to head back?" Connor nodded, stood up and turned shakily, clinging once more to the side of the cliff. Connor had another rest half way and then they were back at the top.

"That was really great! I feel as if I've achieved something."

"I didn't think you'd make it that far. It shows how all your exercising is paying off," Danny remarked. "Has your Dad noticed?"

The joy that filled Connor's face disappeared at the mention of his Dad. "No, he doesn't notice anything I do. He only cares about the fishing."

"I'm sure he cares about you too, he's just..." again his words failed.

"Disappointed in me." Connor finished his sentence bitterly. "He knows I'll never be able to join him in the boat because of my leg!"

"I believe he'll come round one day and realise how talented you are in other ways. He'll be proud of you Connor, I'm sure of it."

"If you're talking about my drawing, forget it. He thinks it's soft and unmanly, not a suitable way for a boy to spend his time." His voice was harsh with resentment.

Danny felt miserable for his friend and didn't know what to say. His own Mum and Dad were always encouraging him, but then he had two good legs and his Dad was not a fisherman, he was a shop keeper not bound by the island tradition and didn't have to be tough like the fishermen.

"Come on Connor, you've done brilliantly today. I'll come by tomorrow and we'll see if you can go a bit further. We'll get you to the beach." Connor gave a bleak smile and taking his friend's outstretched hand got to his feet. He slung his bag containing his paints and sketch book across his shoulder and they walked slowly down the slope together towards the village.

At the bottom they joined the road and saw Moira walking towards them.

"Oh there you are!" she cried. "I wondered where you were. Hi Connor." She glanced briefly in his direction before turning her full attention on Danny.

"Oh Danny, I wish you'd been with us. It was so boring!" She hung onto his arm and gazed up at him with adoring eyes.

"I don't think I would have made much difference. The main Island is boring." He grinned sideways at Connor, raising his eyebrows.

"Well, I can't imagine you had much fun here," she said looking pointedly at Connor. "What did you do anyway?" She began to try to pull ahead walking fast to leave Connor behind, taking Danny with her, but he shook her off and continued to walk with Connor.

"Well you're wrong there," said Danny. "We had a

great time on the top of the cliffs, enjoying the fresh air." He wasn't about to tell her of Connor's ambition to climb down the cliff steps to the beach.

"You're teasing me," she pouted.

"Show her your drawings Connor. Then she'll believe me." Connor frowned, reluctantly pulling out his sketch book and flicking to the last few pages. A black backed gull flew across the page, wings taut against the wind; a bright clump of spikey pink thrift quivered in the breeze; the delicate painting of the harebell, and finally the headland itself with craggy rocks stretching down to a scimitar of golden sand and scattered rock pools, which was the cove itself.

Each painting was breath-taking in its liveliness, but this was lost on Moira.

"Umm, nice, but not very exciting."

"You've got no soul!" Danny chuckled exasperated.

"You go on," Connor said to them. "Don't wait for me. I might go down to the harbour again."

"See you tomorrow," Danny said and walked off up the street with Moira hanging on his arm talking nineteen to the dozen.

CHAPTER 3

The brilliant sunshine of the previous day had disappeared over night to be replaced by low smudgy grey clouds that bowled rapidly across the sky chased by an exuberant wind. A sharp shower of rain rattled against Connor's window as he dressed, disappointed that he wouldn't be able to go up to the cliff-top with Danny and have another go at descending the steps.

The kitchen was warm and stuffy. His mother, Mrs McKenzie, was standing behind the ironing board as usual, with a basket on the sofa piled high with laundry and a stack of ironed garments folded neatly on the dresser.

She was a small woman with dark hair, streaked with grey which she wore pulled back from her face and tied in an untidy bun at the nape of her neck. She was not given to great displays of emotion so appeared to most people as hard and unfeeling, but Connor knew otherwise. He knew her feelings ran very deep, he could see it in her eyes every time his Dad went to sea, which was almost every day; fear and anxiety and a hopeless longing. It was like a knife in Connor's heart to watch, knowing her pain and knowing he could do nothing to comfort her. Mr McKenzie would never give up the sea.

Connor also knew that her anxiety extended to him too. She was terrified of losing him and tried very subtly to keep him close to her. But Connor fought against it causing himself and his mother further pain. She didn't seem to realise that clinging on to him was actually pushing him away. So today was going to be difficult, the weather maybe, forcing him to stay indoors unless he could think of a good reason to go out.

He helped himself to some cereal and sat at the kitchen table.

"Who are you ironing for today?" he asked.

"Mrs Hughes, up at the Big House." The Big House

12

was in fact a converted farm house with a large, expensive extension. It had been bought by a couple who both worked from home. He was a famous writer apparently and she designed clothes for a posh retail chain, so was far too busy to do domestic work. They employed a cleaner and a cook and Connor's mother did their ironing.

"I'll take them up for you," Connor offered. It was a good excuse to escape the house.

"You'll not go out in this weather. That wind's strong enough to blow you over."

Connor huffed. "I can cope! I'm not feeble you know. In fact, my leg is getting stronger every time I use it. You know what they say 'use it or lose it'."

"I don't know why you have to be going out all the time and not happy to stay in doing your drawing and painting."

"I have to go out to find things to draw and paint. There's nothing in here is there?" This wasn't quite true. He'd done several lightning sketches of his mother at the ironing board. He'd never shown them to her, wanting to surprise her on her birthday.

She shook her head. "I just want you to be careful. Don't want you hurting yourself." She straightened up brushing a strand of grey hair from her forehead with the back of her hand. Connor's heart lurched with love for her. She got very little affection from his Dad and now he, Connor, was drifting away from her too. She was a lonely woman.

Connor finished his breakfast then spoke quietly. "I'd like to take them up the hill for you. It's not far and I won't be long. Then I can come back and finish off the sketches I did yesterday."

She pursed her mouth and sighed a sigh of resignation. "Very well. It's a kind offer. I have got a lot more to do for the shop, and the community centre table cloths all need ironing. It would be a help, but you must be careful." She took the pile of garments from the dresser and carefully slid them into a sturdy bag with a wide base and placed them on the table in front of Connor. He rose, and unhitched his waterproof from the back door. Scrambling into it he picked up the bag and went out leaning into the blast that assailed him the moment the door was opened.

He walked down the main street which was completely empty and turned to go up the hill towards the big House at the top. He'd been before and admired the shrubs and flowers that bordered the drive and longed to sketch them; rhododendrons, azaleas thrived in the rich black soil sheltered by high stone walls, a tall Cedar tree with its flat shelf-like branches, and a circular flower bed full of lupins, hollyhocks, huge poppies and masses of white daisies.

He struggled up the hill trying to protect the bag from being buffeted too much. It seemed to get heavier as time went on but he knew this was an illusion. He passed through the gates into the driveway and for a while he walked in the calm provided by the high walls. He limped around to the back of the house, the wind blowing him along now till he reached the shelter of the back door and knocked.

Mrs Hubbard the cook opened the door.

"My Connor what a day to be out! You've brought the ironing I see. Come in, come in and give that leg of yours a rest."

He was ushered in to the roomy kitchen. Large windows with deep windowsills full of flowering geraniums looked out onto a paved area where the washing-line whipped about in the turbulent air. Stainless steel worktops gleamed and saucepans steamed on the huge cooker filling the kitchen with spicy smells.

"Sit yourself down for a moment and get your breath, while I fetch the money for you." She bustled out. The door had been left ajar and Connor could hear music playing in the distance, not the strident tones of popular music but something smooth and gentle like the flowing of a stream Connor thought. Then Mrs Hubbard was back clutching the notes in her hand.

"Ten pounds your Mum said, "is that right?"

"Yes I think so." He stuffed the money into the pocket of his waterproof.

"Would you like a hot drink before you go, to warm you up for the journey back?"

"Thank you, could I have just a drink of water please? The wind dries you out."

She filled a tumbler from the tap.

"And how's that leg of yours?"

He smiled at her "It's getting stronger," he replied confidently.

"Good for you Connor!" She ruffled the top of his head and took the empty glass from him. "It's good to see you helping your Mum."

"Thank you for the drink," he said as he opened the door and limped out into the yard.

He had the wind at his back on the way home, so was able to move more quickly, although on occasions, the force almost blew him over as he couldn't move fast enough to keep up with it. As he reached home the rain began to lash down in sheets again, plastering his hair to his head and trickling down his neck as he couldn't keep his hood up because of the wind.

CHAPTER 4

There were more stacks of neat ironing on the dresser when he got back but his mother was still sliding the iron back and fore over white table cloths this time. The pile in the basket had diminished in size.

Connor handed his mother the money then settled himself at the table, rummaged in his bag taking out his paints and brushes and jar of water.

"Where's my sketch book?" He looked up puzzled.

"I told you I'd look at your drawings," his mother answered her mouth tight and hard.

"What's the matter then?" He asked, hearing the stiffness of her voice. "Didn't you like them?"

"It's not that. I think they're very clever." She paused. "But you've been up to the cliff top haven't you? You could only have done the picture of the cove from there, and I have forbidden you to go anywhere near the top of the cliffs. What would happen if you went too near the edge and your leg gave out or you lost your balance? You'd be over the edge in no time." She thumped the iron down angrily on the table cloth and swished it expertly across the fabric smoothing out all the wrinkles.

Connor felt his own anger rising like a tide. "I don't sit near the edge! No-one in their right mind would go near edge. Just because I've got a useless leg doesn't make me stupid!"

"I'm not saying that. I'm saying you disobeyed me. You're supposed to stay in the village."

But the tide of anger rising in Connor spilt out, flooding the tiny kitchen. "You can't keep me tied to your apron strings forever. I'm fourteen! I'm trying to make a life for myself in spite of my wretched leg. I can't stay cooped up with you forever. I want to get to a point where people don't even notice my leg but notice something else about me instead. All people see is the boy with a limp!

16

I'm fed up with it all. I'm going out!"

He picked up his bag stuffing everything inside, including his sketch book which he found on the arm of the sofa, and grabbing his wet waterproof once more slammed out of the house. He could hear his mother's protests but ignored them as he turned his steps towards the cliff path once more.

***

He reached the top in record time, his anger lending him speed. The wind was still howling but the clouds were marching swiftly away and a pale sun shone sporadically onto the grass which glittered like jewels in its light.

Connor flung himself down in the lee of a large rock. He didn't take out his book, knowing it could be whipped out of his hands. He just sat and gazed trying to calm down. The wind and the waves matched what was going on inside him exactly... the roaring and the turbulence.

He covered his face with his hands pressing his fingers against his eyes which threatened tears. Over and over in his head he could hear all the things he had said. They were all true, but sounded so cruel and ungrateful. He so wanted his mother to understand and help him. He didn't want to battle with her, maybe shut doors for ever. He wanted her to be on his side helping him to make his way to more independence, like other boys of his age. Some went to the main Island on their own, catching the ferry there and back with no problem. He sighed... but he was not allowed out of the village!

The wind was beginning to die down so he shuffled round to gaze out to sea and watch the breakers crashing against the headland. Could he manage a few of the steps on his own he wondered. He could always sit down if the going was too rough. He hitched his bag across his shoulder and made his way slowly to the top of the steps, his heart thumping uncomfortably in his chest.

He gripped the rail tightly as he tentatively stretched out his good leg first before moving his shorter leg. Then repeated the process for the next step until he came to the first place where the rail was missing. He sat down carefully and holding onto the cliff side slid onto the next few steps until the rail was there again. In this way he got as far as the day before. He was immensely pleased with himself.

It was then that he saw the girl again. She was pushing her way through the waves towards the beach, dragging something dark and heavy which she flung down onto the sand as soon as she reached the beach. So she did swim round from the other side of the headland. Then she was off, turning expert cartwheels and running across the sand in complicated patterns, going back and examining her footsteps. Connor watched fascinated and tugging out his sketch pad, began to draw.

He soon had a whole page of her; dancing, twirling, skipping, turning cartwheels and later bending, peering into pools. She was dark-skinned and dressed in a grey dress of some sort. Her hair, though quite short and straight, flew about her head and, as far as he could see was dark brown or black.

Fancy swimming around the headland in that long dress Connor thought. And then, another thought entered his head... he'd never seen her at school so she must have just come to the island, but he hadn't heard of any new people moving into the island. He was puzzled. He'd have to ask around when he got back. New arrivals were a cause for celebration as too many youngsters grew up and moved to the mainland these days.

He decided to try and navigate the crumbled steps, sitting down and holding the cliff face. The first one was fine, and the second, but the third was trickier, the cliff face was smooth and he couldn't grip it so well but he succeeded and felt a rush of triumph. The girl was still there dancing around playing some sort of game, gazing at her shadow now the sun was shining brightly. Connor stood up and descended a few more steps. He was about half way down now and then he heard a shout. The girl heard it too and ran towards the sea, grabbing up the garment she had dropped, and diving expertly beneath the waves. Looking up, Connor saw Danny making his way carefully but speedily down the steps.

"What do you think you're doing?" He exclaimed. "Why didn't you wait for me? I said I'd come."

Connor puffed out his cheeks, breathing out slowly. "The rain and everything. I wasn't sure. And I had a row with my Mum."

Danny scratched his head. "Did you get all this way on your own?"

"I sat down at the difficult bits," Connor admitted.

"That's amazing! You've done really well. Are you fit enough to get back though?"

"I'd better be." Connor laughed. "Can't stay here all night." He heaved himself upright and holding the rail followed Danny up till they came to the crumbled steps, then Danny had to help Connor navigate them safely. The rest of the climb seemed easy to Connor now.

CHAPTER 5

By the time they reached the top, the wind had died down and the sun was shining once again. They perched on the rock side by side.

Danny took a chocolate bar from out of his jacket pocket, broke a piece off and handed it to Connor.

"Did you see her?" Connor asked turning to his friend and taking the chocolate.

"See who?" Danny asked puzzled.

"The girl, on the beach. I've seen her before. She swims into the cove from around the headland."

"Are you sure you're not seeing things? A girl... swimming around the headland...? Even when it's as calm as a mill pond, you can't swim round the headland. It's too dangerous."

"Well how else did she get there? She didn't have a boat. You did see her?"

"Actually Connor, no, I didn't. I was too busy staring at you and how far down the steps you'd managed to get on your own."

"Well she was there. Look, I'll show you." Connor pulled his sketch book from his bag and showed Danny the drawings, who gazed at them in silence.

"She's wearing a dress! She wouldn't be able to swim in that! Are you sure you weren't dreaming?" He gave Connor a worried look. Connor shook his head frowning. He was obviously irritated.

"Where did she go then?" Danny asked handing the sketch book back.

"She dived back into the waves when she heard you shout, you know, just like the seals do when they're scared, although she didn't lumber down the beach, she ran full pelt into the sea and then dived."

"Is that why you're so anxious to reach the beach?" Danny asked grinning. "You want to meet this girl."

Connor tossed his head and punched him on the arm.

"That's not the reason. You know that."

"It does make it more interesting though doesn't it... Mysterious girl on beach? We'll have to find out who she is."

"D'you think she might be staying up at the Big House with Mr and Mrs Hughes?"

"Maybe," said Danny thoughtfully, breaking off some more chocolate and handing another piece to Connor. "Anyway, why didn't you wait for me? What did you row with your Mum about?"

Connor stared out to sea frowning slightly then sighed.

"She saw my sketch of the cove and knew I'd been up here. She's always said I mustn't come up here, it's too dangerous, I might fall over the edge blah! blah! blah!" He was angry again. "All she wants is for me to stay in the village or even better at home with her all the time! I told her I wasn't going to be tied to her apron strings, and slammed out of the house." He finished his tirade. "Came up here." His voice soft now.

"It's 'cos she cares about you Connor. She's afraid for you."

"Well, I can't stand it. It's bad enough coping with all the things I can't do, without being stopped from doing the things I can."

"So what are you going to do?"

"I'm going to carry on, coming up here and I'm going to get down to the beach. I won't tell her about that though, she might lock me up." A faint smile flickered around his mouth.

"Well I won't say anything and I'll help you." They grinned at each other.

***

21

Connor was very reluctant to return home. He'd missed his lunch and he knew he'd upset his mother, but he was determined not to give in and had no intention to stay in the village as his mother wanted. He pushed open the back door. The kitchen was full of the fragrant smell of baking. His mother was bending at the open oven door bringing out a tray of small currant buns. A large fruit cake stood on the wire rack to cool. She set the buns down and turned to face Connor.

"I suppose you've been up to the cliff top again," she said, her lips tight with disapproval.

"Yes Mum. I'm not going to stay in the village all the time. I like to get away from the village. Up there, I'm not reminded of my leg all the time. I lose myself in my drawing, and it makes me happy. I'm sorry it makes you unhappy though."

"Well Connor I can see that nothing I can say will change your mind. You've reached the age where you want to be more independent and I won't try to stop you anymore. But it won't stop me from worrying." She paused. "There's some soup left if you want any."

Connor helped himself to a bowl and poured the soup in carefully from the saucepan that was simmering on the stove, took two slices of bread from the bread bin and sat himself down at the table.

"Have the Hughes at the Big House got people staying with them?" Connor asked his Mum.

"I don't think so. Why d'you ask?"

"I thought I saw someone that I'd not seen before." He shrugged. "It's not important." He scraped up the last remnants of the soup.

"Do you think you could deliver another bag of ironing for me? Or are you too tired?"

"I'm not tired, where do I have to go?"

"It's just Colonel Bannister's few shirts down by the harbour."

"How much?"

"Three pounds fifty."

"I might stay and do some more sketching as it's stopped blowing a gale."

CHAPTER 6

Colonel Bannister was rather deaf, so Connor had to ring the bell twice. He took his freshly ironed laundry and paid Connor what he owed.

The harbour was bustling with life. Some small boats had come in with a fairly decent catch. They were unloading, the gulls screaming and diving. Connor settled himself on an upturned rowing boat and began to sketch once more, capturing the concentration and economy of movement of the sailors as they swung the boxes full of glittering fish onto the quayside.

He lost himself totally in his drawing and didn't notice the tall man who stood watching him, until his shadow fell across the page. Connor looked up then. The man had craggy features, he was quite thin and wore a baggy suit with a cream open neck shirt. His hair was streaked with grey at his temples and was rather long, sticking out over his jacket collar.

"How long have you been drawing young man? You've got quite an 'eye'." Connor shrugged, he'd not seen this man before on the island. "Sorry, let me introduce myself," the man said formally, holding out his hand. "My name is Hughes. I live at the Big House." They shook hands, Connor realising that this was the famous writer. Mr Hughes settled himself on the boat next to Connor. "Well?" He wanted an answer.

"I've always drawn things," Connor replied. "As far back as I can remember."

"Can I see the rest of your sketches?"

Connor handed him his book. Mr Hughes studied each drawing intently, turning the pages back and fore.

"And are you going to do something with it?" he asked, handing the book back. "Or are you going to be a fisherman?"

Connor blushed. "I can't be a fisherman," he replied

24

dropping his gaze. "I have something wrong with my leg." He was bright red by now and very uncomfortable, talking like this to a complete stranger.

The sharp blue eyes of Mr Hughes continued to stare, observing Connor's downcast face, till Connor looked up again.

"With talent like yours lad, I'd be very glad indeed not to have to go to sea." Connor's eyes flew wide, his mouth slightly open in surprise. "Have you ever studied any great paintings?"

"No," he managed to stutter out.

"Come up to the house. You can use my library. It would be good for you to see how the Masters did it. Tomorrow afternoon at about two." He rose to go, then stopped. "What's your name by the way?"

"Connor," Connor replied. Mr Hughes nodded.

"Tomorrow then." He turned and walked away.

Connor sat there dazed. No-one had ever before seen his problem with his leg as a good thing. It was a completely new idea to Connor. No-one had ever taken his sketching really seriously before either. It had always been considered like a consolation prize, second best, except for Danny of course, but then he didn't come from a fishing family. Connor felt vaguely excited. Maybe there was something in his drawings after all, a future perhaps.

The wind was getting up again so he put his book away and decided to walk along the harbour and think about what Mr Hughes had said. His father would be coming down to the quayside soon with the rest of his crew to prepare the boat for a night fishing trip. They all had shares in the boat and the profit or losses were divided equally between them all.

Connor didn't want to meet his father. Seeing his Dad always sent him into a spiral of shame and misery and he didn't want his tiny bubble of hope to be burst just yet. He walked as briskly as he could to the far side of the harbour.

The sea was the colour of molten lead and heaved shiny muscles of waves. The boats bobbed and dipped, riding the swell. There were so many gulls in shore that Connor could tell heavy weather was brewing. Clouds were scudding in from the west, banking up in great purple clusters. Dad would have a tough time tonight. Of course, Connor knew, that by midnight it might have blown itself out and a serene calm reign, with a bright moon. He watched as the men came down to the boats, his father among them. There was quite a bit of activity before they set out onto the swelling tide, followed by an excited crowd of gulls, hoping for easy pickings.

He watched the boats till they seemed to disappear where the sky and sea merged into one. Then turned for home.

***

Connor knew he couldn't tell his mother about his encounter with Mr Hughes as he had been so encouraging about his sketches. He sighed, another thing to keep from his family! Still he had told his mother he had no intention of not going to the top of the cliff so, if he went to the Big House he'd let her think he was at the cliff top.

His tea was ready when he got in. He washed his hands and sat at the table.

"Your Dad's set off," his mother commented. "The weather's rough."

"I saw him go," Connor answered.

"Did he see you?"

"No I always keep out of his way."

"It shouldn't be like this," his mother exclaimed. "He's your father!"

"It's not my fault! Talk to him about it. He's the one that's ashamed of me!" He stabbed at a sausage and cut it in half angrily.

"It's not that Connor."

"Oh what is it then?"

"He just doesn't know... how to be."

"You'd have thought he would have worked something out by now. He's had fourteen years!" Connor was tired of the arguments. He always seemed to be falling out with his Mum these days. He was much happier when he was out of the house, but it made him feel bad.

Tea over, he cleared a space on the table and began to colour wash his drawings of the harbour. He was careful to keep the drawings of the girl hidden. He didn't want any more questions. His mother listened to the radio, a classical music channel and took out her knitting. She was knitting a huge, thick jumper for his Dad in brown and grey stripes. The arms seemed to go on forever, but Connor knew by past experience that it would fit his Dad perfectly when it was all sewn up.

This was the only type of evening Connor enjoyed, when the wind was howling outside, but they were tucked away safely in the little stone cottage wrapped around by music that spoke to Connor. Sometimes the music was light and bright like a Spring morning, and sometimes it raged and roared like the worst Winter storms. Tonight it soothed his jangled emotions bringing him a sense of calm and optimism.

CHAPTER 7

Connor woke the next day with a squirm of excitement in his belly. This afternoon he was to go up to the House and look at books in Mr Hughes' library. He didn't consider this a boring occupation as maybe some of the other boys would. It felt like an adventure, as if he would be stepping into a new world.

He arrived at the breakfast table surprised to see his father sitting there drinking a large mug of tea. His father looked at him as he came in and Connor felt the usual surge of shame and misery which he tried to hide.

"Dad you're still up! Was the trip alright?" His voice sounded bright and brittle.

"The storm blew itself out by the time we got to the grounds. The fish were jumping into the nets. We couldn't manage any more so we came home." His Dad's voice was low and rumbled in his chest, his weather-beaten face heavily lined and almost mahogany in colour, his hair, stiff with salt was white as snow, and his hands were large and calloused; strong, competent hands. He was a lot older than Connor's mother.

"A good catch then?"

"They'll fetch a fair price. And what've you been doing?" The question Connor dreaded. He sighed.

"Not much. Helped Mum by delivering the ironing."

"He's been up the cliff top," his mother chipped in. Connor gave her a black look.

"Have you now?" His Dad's eyebrows inched up to his hair line.

"And what were you doing up there?"

Suddenly Connor felt his anger rising once more and a new boldness filled his being. Maybe his conversation with Mr Hughes had something to do with it. He raised his head and looked his Dad squarely in the eyes.

"You know very well what I've been doing. I've been

drawing! It's not something I'm going to be ashamed of anymore. I'm good, I've got a talent and I'm going to use it. Who knows how far I can go with it, college, university even. Just because I can't be a fisherman like you doesn't make me a useless person!" His face was red, his breath coming in tight gasps. His father looked away in disgust.

"We're a fishing family. Have been for generations!"

"Well, it stops with me! You'll have to get used to it!" His father half rose from the table, his fist raised and his face like thunder. A stifled cry from Connor's mother caused him to pause and he sat down again, lifting his mug and taking a huge slurp of his tea still staring at Connor over the rim.

"You might have a gammy leg but you're growing up, developing some back-bone I'll give you that, but I'll not take any more cheek from you, do you understand that?"

"Yes Father," But Connor's gaze was steady, his head erect.

***

Connor spent the morning in his room putting the finishing touches to his drawings of the girl, remembering the soft grey of her dress and the darkness of her skin. He left as soon as lunch was over, which had been a silent affair with his Dad glowering at him from the other end of the table.

"Where are you off to now?" His mother asked. Connor froze, he didn't want to tell them about Mr Hughes.

"Just out."

"Can you deliver some more ironing for me?"

"Yeah sure. Where to?"

"Mrs Robertson. She must be doing Spring cleaning again. I've had two pairs of curtains to iron. They won't be too heavy for you to carry will they?"

"No," Connor took the bag and swung it to feel its weight. "Fine. How much?"

"Six pounds. They were big curtains."

Mrs Robertson lived at the opposite side of the village to the Big House, but as he had left home so early, he had plenty of time to deliver the ironing.

She came to the door red faced, obviously very busy.

"Oh Connor your mother's a godsend. I've got visitors coming tomorrow and I'm getting their rooms ready. How much do I owe you?"

"Mum said six pounds." She went to fetch her purse and pressed a five pound note and two pound coins into Connor's hand. He looked up surprised.

"That's a pound for you... for being the delivery boy."

Connor smiled happily. "Thank you Mrs Robertson."

He decided to make his way straight to the Big House, and not pop into the shop and spend his pound. He would save it.

***

When he reached the Big House Connor went to the front door not the back. He didn't want Mrs Hubbard gossiping about his visit. Even though he knew she would eventually find out and her gossiping would reach his mother's ears. He didn't want to think about what would happen then.

The front door was opened by Mr Hughes himself.

"Come in, come in Connor. Would you like some tea? Or lemonade perhaps?"

Connor shook his head feeling suddenly very shy in this huge house. "Nothing thank you," he managed to stammer.

"This way then." Mr Hughes walked swiftly along the wide hall-way then stopped and flung open a door on their right and looked back at Connor as he came limping after him. His forehead creased in a frown.

"What is the problem with your leg?" He gave Connor a penetrating stare.

Connor stopped. He hadn't had to explain about his leg for a long time, everybody knew. "I was born with one leg shorter than the other."

"Umm, shame. Doesn't stop you drawing though, does it?" He ushered Connor into the big room. Three of the walls were lined with book shelves. Every shelf crammed with books. The fourth wall seemed to be made out of windows from floor to ceiling, which looked out onto the garden. Not at all the garden that Connor would have expected so grand a house to have. It was more like a meadow, stretching away to a spinney of small trees at the far end. The grass which had once been lawns, was semi-wild and long, with wild flowers blooming in it; Ox-eye daisies, Buttercups, and pink Clover.

The grass was bordered with hedges of Rhododendrons that were covered in white flowers. Lilac Field Bindweed and Clematis scrambled over it adding colour. Beneath the hedges were clumps of pink and white Campion, spiky purple Persicaria and a splash of bright red Poppies. Connor stared in delight, itching to go out and draw. A voice interrupted his reverie.

"I've looked out some books for you and put them on the table here." Connor turned from the window and made his way to where the books lay. Several with glossy illustrations of famous paintings were open on the table. One was black and white drawings of religious scenes mostly, but turning the page he found animals and birds in exquisite detail.

"The artist's name is Durer." Connor was informed. "A great draughtsman. This of course is Da Vinci." Mr Hughes continued, pulling forward another great tome. "You've heard of him?" Connor nodded. Mr Hughes

31

heaved a huge sigh. "Well Connor I'll leave you to it. You can browse as much as you like. The Art section is over there," he said pointing to a section of shelves by the window.

CHAPTER 8

The rest of the afternoon flew by. Connor picked his way through the illustrations, fascinated by the different styles and subjects. Some pictures he thought were horrible and he skipped past these quickly, others he thought rather rude, not used to looking at naked men and women. But he was interested in the water colour seascapes of someone called Copley Fielding and he loved the way he painted the skies.

After a while, Mr Hughes came in carrying a tray with a jug of lemonade and a glass, a teapot and a cup and saucer and a plate of biscuits.

"I thought you might like some refreshments after all," he said, putting the tray down on a low coffee table in front of a large comfy sofa. "Come and sit and tell me which Artists you like best. You see, Connor, I believe you could go to Art college or university. You have a talent." He poured himself a cup of tea and a glass of lemonade for Connor. "Help yourself to biscuits."

Connor was silent for a moment trying to take in what Mr Hughes had just said about university, then, fetching a few books from the big table and balancing them carefully on his knee, showed Mr Hughes the paintings he most admired and how much he liked the way they depicted the landscape.

"Would you like to visit again and bring your pencils and paints and maybe copy some of their compositions and the way they use colour? Do you think you would learn something from it?"

"I would love to try and get the cloud effects. You can almost feel the wind in some of the paintings."

Mr Hughes smiled. "I know what you mean."

"I would also love to draw some of the flowers in your garden." Connor spoke up boldly. "There aren't many different flowers up on the clifftop, and you've got so many."

"That's my wife's passion. She hates things to be too formal and loves things to look as natural as possible. When we moved in the garden had been totally neglected and my wife loved it and refused to employ a gardener to tame it. She takes care of it now but mostly leaves it to do its own thing."

Connor noticed the time on the library clock. "I think I ought to go now," he said rising to his feet. "It's nearly my teatime. Thank you so much for showing me your books."

Mr Hughes stood up too and walked to the front door with Connor. "I'm very pleased you enjoyed your visit. So you'd like to come again? Same time next week? Don't forget your paints." He shook Connor's hand as they said goodbye.

Connor walked down the drive turning everything over in his head. He'd been afraid that Mr Hughes would be cold and superior rather too 'posh' for his liking with his cut-glass English accent, but as they talked together sharing biscuits Connor realised that in fact he was a rather shy man and seemed almost afraid to share his enthusiasm for painting. Connor decided he liked him and his heart lifted when he remembered that he'd been invited to visit again.

He reached home in time to lay the table for tea. He gave his mother the money from Mrs Robertson and helped dish up, then carried the plates to the table just as his Dad came in.

His father sat at the head of the table and waited for his wife to sit down before starting the meal. They discussed the fishing and its future. In spite of the large catch they'd just had, on the whole the trend was down. His father blaming the increase of the seal population and huge industrial boats that caught tons of fish at a time.

Connor let the conversation wash over him. He'd heard it all before. After tea his father went out to The

Bluebell pub to join his crew for a drink and his mother settled in her chair with the radio playing softly and continued her knitting.

"Where were you all afternoon?" she asked Connor. "You didn't take your painting bag."

"I just wandered around thinking, looking at stuff."

"Danny came looking for you. He had that girl Moira with him."

"I'm glad he didn't find me." Connor frowned. "She can't stand me, and I can't stand her."

"I fret for you sometimes Connor. Why haven't you made more friends? You always seem to be on your own."

"You know why Mum. I can't join in their games. So even if they ask me now I just say no, it's simpler. I don't mind being on my own. Most of the things I enjoy doing you can't share. Drawing is not a team sport." That brought the conversation to an end. He fetched his bag from upstairs and spread his things out on the kitchen table and continued to finish off some of his sketches from memory.

***

Connor spent the next morning delivering some of his mother's ironing. She'd been worried at first that it would be too much for him and cause his leg to ache or bring on the nagging back-ache, but when he protested loudly that he liked doing it and it was good for him, she gave in.

The islanders were a generous people and appreciated Connor helping his Mum out and began to give him tips, fifty pence or a pound. He had decided to save up for a new water colour pad with paper which wouldn't crinkle when it was wet. The one he was using was almost finished.

After lunch he took his painting bag and set off for the

cliff top once more, determined to practise climbing down the steps again, going a bit further each day. This time he reached the patch of crumbling steps much more quickly and manoeuvred his way past them with relative ease. The bottom of the steps was so much closer now and the sand wide and inviting. He pushed himself further on, remembering that he had to have enough energy to climb back up. He stopped with a sigh. Tomorrow he promised himself, he would reach the sand.

He twisted round and began the long climb back up to the cliff top. When he stopped for a rest and looked up to check how much further he had to go, Danny was sitting on the topmost step. He waved at Connor.

"You're doing really well. You'll soon reach the beach. Do you want me to give you a hand or are you OK?"

Connor grinned. "I'm fine thanks." He pressed on moving up step by step with increasing confidence. He was quite breathless when he reached the top and sat panting beside his friend sucking in his breath.

"We're having a games night tonight, just wondered if you'd like to come. Mum and Dad are out for the evening, said I could have a few friends round, as long as we don't wreck the place."

"I'm up for that. Will Moira be coming?"

"Not tonight. I thought you and Rory and Ewan."

"What time shall I come round?"

"About seven thirty or eight. Rory's bringing his new board game to try. Hopefully you won't win all the time like you usually do. Have you got enough energy to walk down to Gaelcreags?"

Gaelcreags was a large village, almost a town, on the other side of the headland. Very picturesque and the haunt of the more adventurous tourists, mostly arty types who liked to paint the rugged landscape. The two boys followed the path that ran beside the cliff edge and wound down amongst the out-lying stone houses and small rundown barns that housed a few chickens and sheep in the wild Winter months.

The main street contained shops that sold souvenirs and postcards, a few coffee shops and cafes, an Art shop that sold everything an artist might require, a toy shop, a book shop as well as the usual food and clothes shops.

Connor gazed into the Art shop window to find out the price of a water-colour sketch book...eight pounds for one of medium size. He frowned. It would take a while for him to save up enough to buy one. Danny wanted to look in the toy shop as they sold board games, to see what they had. They browsed the games but there was nothing to take Danny's fancy so they ended up having a coke in the cafe. Connor told Danny about Mr Hughes and his afternoon at the Big House. Danny was surprised.

"I don't think I've ever seen him, or her for that matter. They're both like a pair of hermits. What's he like?"

"He was very nice," Connor replied. "He's got a huge library, floor to ceiling shelves, crammed with all sorts of books and he'd put all these Art books out for me to look at. We had drinks and biscuits and he wants me to go again."

"D'you want to go again?" Danny couldn't imagine anyone getting excited about Art books.

"Yes, I do." Connor dropped his gaze, looking down at the table. "He thinks I could go to college or university," he said in a low voice.

Danny's eyes widened in surprise, not many youngsters from the village went to university, especially not a fisherman's son.

"How are you going to do that? And what would your Dad say?"

Connor instantly realised he could have made a mistake sharing this information with Danny. "Please Danny don't say anything to anybody. I haven't given it much thought.

37

He was probably just being kind. You won't say anything will you?"

"Not if you don't want me to. I can't imagine your Dad being very pleased."

"Nor me," Connor sighed. "We'd better get back." They left the cafe and set off for home.

CHAPTER 9

That evening Connor arrived at Danny's house a bit after seven thirty. The other lads had already arrived and were sitting around the big square dining room table, the board set out, the cards and pieces assembled. He sat in the vacant chair that had been provided and studied the board while Rory explained the rules and how to play it. The game involved trains and tracks and destinations across the world.

As the evening wore on the banter and rivalry increased. Normally, in the familiar board games, Connor stormed ahead and was often the winner, but tonight he wasn't concentrating and easily let good opportunities pass him by. Ewan shouted and punched the air when he won for the third time in a row.

"Makes a change Connor for someone else to win," Ewan said. "Mind you it's to do with travelling. You don't do that so well." His attempt at humour fell flat and was followed by an uncomfortable silence.

But Connor gave a smile. "I think I'd manage a train. Walking's not my thing." Everyone smiled then, and the moment passed. But Ewan bolstered by his success began to talk about beginning to work on the boat with his father.

"I'll soon be going with them. Dad says I'll make a great fisherman. I'm as good as the others just about, and it won't be long. I'm really useful and he's proud of the way I muck in. A chip off the old block like my brothers, Tom and Duncan. It'll be great the whole family going to sea together."

"I'm not sure I want to be a fisherman," Rory chipped in. "And Dad's not sure I'm quite ready yet. He says he'd like me to follow in his footsteps but I'm not sure. Mum wants me to do something with my education. But you know what I'm like, learning stuff and passing exams is so boring. I reckon I'd do better going to sea."

"Well I don't mind following my old man and running a grocer's shop. It's a good life with no danger of drowning!" Danny declared. They all laughed and turned to Connor.

He pulled a face and shrugged. "I guess I'll have to wait and see. Maybe I'll help you in your shop Danny."

"I think you might surprise us all, with your drawing and stuff," Danny retorted. Connor coloured and sent Danny a dagger of a look.

"Oh yeah!" scoffed Ewan. "One day someone will 'talent spot' him and he'll be a famous artist! Not on this island mate." He grinned around at the others but they didn't grin back. There was another uncomfortable pause.

"Come on," said Danny, breaking the momentary tension. "Let's play cards." He found the pack in the table drawer and began to deal. They played 'Cheat' and 'Black Jack' the usual friendly banter restored. When Danny's parents arrived home, the little party broke up.

"See you tomorrow Connor," Danny called as Connor walked down the road home.

***

The tide was right in on Thursday morning. The big breakers thumping into the cliffs like battering-rams. The loud crack as the waves hit, sounding like gun-fire. The spray fountained into the air... great lacy curtains seeming to hang still for a moment before cascading down into the creamy foam beneath.

Connor loved the wildness of the sea, the waves boiling and swirling like a turbulent cauldron, as much as he loved the peaceful blue skies and the gentle strength of harebells.

He sat on the top step and gazed down mesmerized at the violence of the water and the imperturbable rock of the cliff face. The sea like a furious child raging against a tall implacable father. But he also knew that as time passed the sea would win, gradually wearing away the rock face and causing the cliff to crumble and fall.

He sighed deeply. Taking out his sketch book and pencils, he began to draw. This time, he let his imagination wander. Small fists emerged from the waves beating ineffectually against the cliff which reared heavenward clothed in the tall boots and wide waterproof garb of the fisherman whose granite features stared out across the sea. Connor studied what he had done then suddenly smiled and began to fill in more detail.

**

After lunch he went back up to the cliff top. The tide would be out, but it never completely left the cove. The beach shelved steeply and the sea swirled around the two headlands imprisoning the tiny beach.

Today Connor was going to reach that beach and explore the rock pools drawing whatever he could find. If Danny arrived, he could join him. He'd manage the steps easily.

He set off down the steps more confidently, but being sensible and holding the rail firmly. When he reached the crumbled steps, he slowed down and hung on to the cliff side making sure his foot was safely placed before putting his whole weight upon it. As he neared the end he could see that the steps had been worn away to form a bumpy ramp, by the constant wash and thump of the sea. The rail had rusted away. So, clinging to the cliff wall he walked gingerly down the incline. Then as the cliff face curved away from the slope, careered down the final stretch, and rolled over in the sand, laughing and gasping by turns. He had achieved his goal.

Connor stood up, brushing the damp sand from his

jeans. He wanted to run and skip and dance like the girl he had seen. So he limped around in a circle as fast as he could, opening his arms wide, embracing the cove, the cliffs and the sea, in one huge gesture of joy. He stopped, panting, gazing towards the rock pools, his face alight with happiness.

"Why do you walk like that?"

Connor froze and turned around slowly. The girl was standing behind him. Water dripped from her clothes forming a shiny patch of wet sand around her feet. Her hair which was plastered to her head, was shiny too, like seaweed.

"Where did you come from?" It was a stupid question, but he was too shocked to say anything sensible. She just looked back at the sea then looked at him. Then repeated her question.

Connor swallowed. He hated talking about his leg, but she was waiting for an answer.

"I was born with one leg shorter than the other. It makes me limp."

Her face didn't soften with sympathy. She replied in a very matter-of-fact tone. "That's the trouble with land. It wouldn't matter in the sea... I saw you come down the steps. It's hard for you isn't it?"

Connor nodded staring at her in her strange grey clothes which hung in loose soggy folds about her body. Her face was round, her eyes were huge and a very deep liquid brown. Her hair was short and cut straight just beneath her ears and hung down on either side of her face like thick curtains.

"Did you really swim round the point dressed like that?"

"What else would I wear?"

"Well… a swimsuit. Something that doesn't drag at you in the water."

"These don't drag when I'm in the water. Anyway why

42

was it so important for you to come to the beach?" She walked towards him closing the distance between them.

"I'm not sure really... I hate not being able to do things like the other boys and I know they wouldn't dream of coming down here because it's so dangerous. I suppose I wanted to prove to myself that there are things I can do too."

"What's in your bag?" She asked pointing.

"You're full of questions aren't you?" Connor retorted, slightly irritated at the way she switched subjects all the time.

"I'm interested, that's all."

He opened his bag and brought out his sketch book and pencils.

"Let me see!" she leant forward eagerly as he opened up the book.

"We'd better sit down somewhere out of the wind." Connor looked around and began to move towards the large rocks at the base of the cliff. She skipped beside him occasionally turning a cartwheel and dancing off then running back to catch him up.

They settled side by side on a large flat rock in the shelter of the high cliffs.

CHAPTER 10

The strange girl stared in delight at the drawings and traced them tentatively with a hesitant finger. The birds she recognised easily, but gave them odd names that Connor had never heard before. The flowers, she was not familiar with at all.

"What are these called?" she asked pointing at a clump of pink thrift.

"Thrift," Connor replied. "Have you not seen them before?"

She shook her head, then laughed when the next page revealed a Puffin with a beak-full of eels. She muttered something unintelligible.

"We call them Puffins," Connor told her. The girl laughed again and repeated what he said.

She sat stock still pulling back a little when he turned the page, seeing herself dancing, skipping and cartwheeling across the white expanse of paper.

"But... that is me," she said in amazement. "When? How?" Her face a picture of puzzlement and wonder. Connor smiled sideways at her.

"I've seen you a couple of times, and last time, when I was on the steps I drew you."

"One day you will be a great painter! You have a magic pencil!" she declared.

"Not really," Connor replied shaking his head. "It comes with practice. Anyway," he said shutting the book and changing the subject. "Where do you come from? You don't live on this island do you? Are you staying with relatives?"

"I come from another island. My name is Morag, it means princess, you know."

"I know what it means," he replied impatiently. "But which island d'you come from? The nearest one is about twenty miles away and you couldn't swim that distance in this sea." Connor retorted. "I know! You're on a boat and swam in from the boat."

"Maybe," she said getting up and skipping away from him. "Why don't you come down to the sea with me. We could swim together, dive in and out of the waves." She held out her arms to him beckoning, urging.

Connor shook his head. "I can't swim. My parents would never let me go into the sea because it's dangerous and my leg is weak, and especially in this cove because the beach shelves so steeply. The water's very deep and the currents are strong."

Morag walked back up the beach towards him her arms hanging loosely by her sides, her face creased with concern.

"That is so sad. The sea is full of life. You would be strong in the sea. I can teach you to swim. I am a very good swimmer. You would be safe with me," she assured him, and took his hand giving it a little tug. He rose reluctantly and they walked towards the sea together.

"I can't go in with my clothes on. I could paddle though if I take my trainers off." Connor knelt on the sand to undo his laces and rolled up the legs of his jeans. He noticed what looked like a large grey coat in a heap at the water's edge.

"Is that yours?" he asked, nodding in the coat's direction.

"Yes," she said absently, watching carefully what Connor was doing. "What's that in your shoe?" She asked, pointing at the heavy insole in one of his trainers.

"It's the insole I have to wear to help balance my legs. It's not very good though, but I do walk better with it in my shoe." He stepped onto the sand, leaning heavily to one side. The toes of his right leg, which was a good inch shorter than his left, just reaching the sand.

Morag watched him taking tentative limping steps towards the water, then walked resolutely by his side.

"Lean on me if you like, I'm strong."

"I want to do it myself."

"Fine." But she didn't leave his side.

The water was icy cold. Connor gasped and staggered, but managed to right himself. The waves were no bigger than ripples at the edge and further out the water was as still as a millpond. He could feel the sandy floor falling away steeply beneath his freezing toes. The edge of his jeans was soon wet, even though he'd rolled them up to his knees. He stopped not willing to get any wetter. Morag was out in deep water swimming and diving, reminding him of dolphins and seals… so at home in the water. She came towards him as he turned back to the beach.

"What is your name?" she asked. "I can't just call you boy."

Connor half-turned towards her, missed his footing and fell with an enormous splash. He tried to get up but the sea kept washing over him. He spluttered, spitting out the salty water and began to laugh, sitting in the sand absolutely soaked. Morag joined him in the shallows splashing down beside him, laughing too.

"So much for trying to keep dry and not swimming in my clothes!" Connor said when he managed to stop laughing. "My name is Connor, by the way."

"Nice to meet you Connor," said Morag standing up and offering him her hand. He took it and she pulled him to his feet. "Now I have to go. Next time, bring your swimsuit and we will swim and keep your clothes dry."

"Next time?"

"Yes, the tide is just right the afternoons so we can meet up on the beach. I'll teach you to swim." Connor grinned at her, knowing he was breaking all the parental rules, but in doing so feeling stronger and more positive about himself.

"OK you're on," he replied, his face wreathed in smiles. Morag stooped and gathered up the big grey garment and ran into the water diving into the sea-green depth and disappearing.

Connor sat on the sand and put his trainers back on, then made his way up the beach towards the steps. He was extremely tired by the time he got to the top and had to have a few stops on the way. He looked out to sea and could see a family of seals just rounding the headland, bobbing about and diving smoothly beneath the glassy swell of the sea.

He sat down on his favourite rock, his thoughts in a whirl. So many new things were happening to him at the moment; meeting Mr Hughes, the suggestion of studying Art seriously at a college or university, meeting Morag, the possibility of learning to swim and the overall sudden feeling of freedom, making decisions for himself. He was excited and a little scared. Two futures stood before him, the safe stay-at-home life where other people made decisions for him, or the open door to an unknown future, but one he could write himself. He liked the idea of the open door and hoped it would not be shut in his face. He gazed at the horizon where the sea met the sky... a barrier or a border? It was a border now and he was determined to cross it.

"Hey Connor!" Danny's shout brought him back from his day-dreaming. He waved and waited. As Danny came closer he stared at the state of Connor's clothing. "What have you been up to? You're soaking wet. You've been on the beach haven't you? And in the sea by the look of it." He chuckled, eyes sparkling, mouth in a wide grin. "What's come over you Connor? You've always been a bit on the timid side, but you're changing!"

"I know, it's something Mr Hughes said about being grateful for my disability, because I can now think of doing something different, not concentrating on what I can't do, like joining Dad on the boat." He shrugged. "I feel more confident - hopeful even." Danny gave him a playful thump on the arm.

"Good for you. I hope everything works out. You'll have some battles ahead."

"Yeah, but I'm not bothered about it. I'm determined to give it my best shot. I'm not staying on this island forever. I'm going to make a life for myself somewhere else."

"You'd better get dry before you go home. Your Mum's bound to guess what you've been up to. I can't believe you went into the sea! It's so dangerous!"

"I only went paddling, but fell over. It was funny really." He laughed remembering how he and Morag had laughed together. He was not going to tell Danny about Morag. He didn't want to share this friendship with anyone. She was his secret.

The afternoon sun was very warm and the two boys decided to walk over to Gaelcreags again. Connor asked how things were between Danny and Moira and was surprised to see Danny blush.

"We're getting on fine. I know she can be a bit sharp. But I really like her. The more I've got to know her... you know."

"Good. As long as she makes you happy. I thought you might prefer Fiona."

"She's too shy for me."

"I guess most of the gang are going to start pairing up now."

"D'you like any of the girls in particular?"

"Na! I'm not really interested and anyway," Connor added "No-one's going to want to go out with someone who limps along like me." Connor wasn't looking for sympathy, he'd come to this conclusion a long time ago and it was just a fact as far as he was concerned. Now friendship was another thing altogether. He would like more friends but always held back fearing their pity. Danny was the only one who treated him the same as any of the others. He teased him and argued with him and Connor never felt pitied by him.

By the time they reached Gaelcreags Connor was almost dry and was able to brush the sand off his clothes. They bumped into Rory in the Village centre and the three of them spent the rest of the afternoon, which wasn't long, sitting on the sea wall drinking cans of coke and watching the tourists cluster round Old Geordie. He was an ancient fisherman who told tall tales to the tourists who paid him well for his trouble.

They listened idly as the familiar story drifted to their ears. Geordie was an excellent story teller and the boys found themselves drawn in, in spite of the fact that they'd heard it all before. Today he was telling the story of the Seal-Catcher's Adventure. When he'd finished his audience begged for one more tale so he obliged. Moving his pipe from one side of his mouth to the other he began the sad tale of The Selkie.

Connor's mind drifted back to earlier in the afternoon and the sight of the happy seal family playing together far out in the ocean.

CHAPTER 11

A flat grey sea mist had drifted in overnight, chilling the air and making Connor think of dull November days. The gulls squawked and screamed sounding annoyed and frustrated strutting along the quay-side. A pearly dew clothed the roofs and fences, ledges and benches. But this was early July and Connor knew the sun would soon send its warming rays through the mist and it would be gone, burnt off by lunch time.

He delivered his Mum's ironing in the morning earning himself another one pound fifty. He would soon have enough for a new sketch pad. His thoughts kept turning to the afternoon, his stomach lurching alarmingly with excitement. He was going to launch out into deep water and learn to swim. He had never felt so strong before. He knew he could do it. Luckily Danny was going to be busy all day helping his Dad in the shop so had not arranged to meet up with Connor.

He had a very small lunch, partly excitement but also remembering not to have a heavy meal before swimming.

"Eat up Connor it's not like you to nibble like a mouse. Are you alright?"

"I'm fine Mum, just not hungry. I'll probably eat a big tea." He squeezed himself out from behind the table. "Just going upstairs to get my bag."

"Up to the cliffs again I suppose." His Mum glowered at him. Connor sighed.

"I'm quite safe. I sit on a rock and draw."

He pulled an old pair of shorts on beneath his jeans, and grabbing his bag, he navigated the narrow staircase hurrying as much as possible and trying not to stumble, but he couldn't wait to get out of the house and meet Morag.

As he had suspected, the sun was shining, the gulls screaming across the bright blue sky, the mist gone. Connor reached the top of the cliffs in record time. He purposely slowed and took a deep calming breath before descending the steps. He didn't want to stumble on those.

There was just a fine crescent of shiny wet sand below the cliffs and no sign of Morag. His heart sank in disappointment. He wandered over to the rocks on the far side of the cove kicking at the odd loose pebble in frustration. The rocks were draped elegantly in seaweed, some bright green and fine like hair, others like Bladderwrack, thick and a browny-black with swellings at intervals down the glistening strands, very tough and slippery. He pulled out his sketch book preparing to draw it, capturing the wetness and roundness of the bladders that caused it to float.

"There's no time for that if you want to learn to swim," said the voice behind him.

"How did you manage to creep up on me again?"

Morag shrugged and grinned. She had the big garment which was more like a cape or cloak, slung over her shoulder suspended by a finger. She threw it down on the sand.

"Are you ready then?" She asked looking him up and down.

"I've got my trunks on under my clothes. I won't be a minute." He quickly removed his trainers, jeans and tee shirt, shivering in the cool wind that whipped in from the sea.

"The sea will feel warm once you're in the water," Morag told him.

As they walked towards the sea Morag began to sing to herself. At first Connor couldn't distinguish the words, but as they entered the rippling sea the words came to him. She was singing to the sea, her voice, soft and low, her eyes closed.

I soothe you. I smooth you
Tempestuous sea,

Just wrinkles of ripples
Come softly to me.

Connor couldn't swear to it but, it seemed to him that the huge crashing waves that raced around the headland and surged into the tiny cove of Dernvoe, calmed down. There was certainly a lessening of foam and spray. He gave Morag a quick side-ways glance. Her eyes flew open and she took his hand.

"It begins to slope steeply here," she said. They were wading now knee-deep. The water forcing itself against his legs. Connor struggled and felt fear rising through him.

"Don't be afraid," Morag said as if she could read his mind, and gripping his hand more tightly continued. "See the water as your friend."

"I don't want to go any further!" Connor exclaimed standing stock still, the swell of the sea almost reaching his waist.

"This is fine," Morag assured him her eyes sparkling. "Take both my hands now." He did so and found his feet leave the sandy floor and he was drifting on the surface of the sea propelled by Morag. Every now and then the water filled his mouth and sometimes went up his nose. He spluttered and spat tossing the water out of his face.

Morag stopped pulling him and he felt his foot touch the sand once more.

"You're doing really well. You were made for the sea! This time, you must kick your legs and later, I'll show you how to move your arms." She again took his hands and this time he followed her instructions and kicked his legs vigorously. To his delight it really didn't matter that his right leg was so much shorter. It made no difference at all. He surged through the water losing his grip on Morag's hands, sailed like a torpedo for a few yards then sank, blowing bubbles. She was there in the water beside him, grabbing and pulling him back up into the air. She was laughing.

"You are so confident! Have another go." She took his hands once more, and again Connor moved smoothly through the water kicking his legs as he went. This time he didn't sink, but stopped and gently touched the bottom with his left leg then his right. The water was up to his armpits and he swayed slightly in the currents. Morag steadied him. They continued for a while longer until Connor's teeth began to chatter.

"I'll have to show you how to use your arms and how to float. But I think that's enough for today."

Connor blew the salty wetness from his face and slicked back his dripping hair.

"That was fabulous!" he declared. "You were right it made no difference my leg being short. I'll be able to do what I like in the water!" His face was shining with joy. "I feel 'normal'!" He grabbed her hands once more and she pulled him around in a circle sending waves in all directions.

They made their way up the beach to where Connor had left his clothes. He had managed to sneak a towel into his bag and pulling it out was soon rubbing himself dry. He secured it firmly around his waist and wriggled out of his wet trunks and into his dry clothes.

Morag was wandering around the base of the cliffs squatting down to gaze into the pools and lifting stones to see what was under them.

"Did you know there is a cave here that goes deep into the cliff?" she asked Connor who was drying his hair with the towel and succeeded in turning it into something resembling a bird's nest. He dropped the towel and wandered over to her combing his fingers through his hair to try to straighten it a bit.

"No, no-one's ever mentioned caves."

"I'll show you one day. Will you show me how you draw things?"

"OK what do you want me to draw?"

"This pool with the seaweed."

Connor fetched his bag from where he'd left his clothes and settled on a large rock overlooking the pool. He could see the fleshy fingers of sea anemones, the pointed shells of limpets and the sudden scurry of a crab. Morag squatted beside him watching closely, how he held the pencil, how he narrowed his eyes as he scrutinised the pool and the soft gentle lines he set down on the paper.

"I'll paint it later," he said

"Oh, can't you do it now? It's like magic."

Connor laughed, his insides squirmed with pleasure and a rosy blush stained his cheeks.

"OK, I've got time." He pulled out his jar of water and flipped up the lid of his paints. Taking out a fat brush he laid down a wash of water before choosing a finer brush and painting the individual objects in the pool. The colours blended and smudged together creating a marvellous watery effect.

Morag clapped her hands with enthusiasm. "I'd love to be able to do that!" She exclaimed her eyes shining with delight.

"You can have it if you like," said Connor, preparing to tear the page from his book.

"Oh no, no, no! You keep it for me. I can't take it with me now."

"OK, another time."

"Shall we do more swimming tomorrow?" Morag asked.

"If you don't mind teaching me. I really enjoyed today."

"Tomorrow then."

Connor returned to gather up his towel and swimming trunks and when he looked round to say goodbye, Morag had completely disappeared. He scanned the beach and the sea. All he could see was the head of a lone seal bobbing in and out of the waves.

Connor wandered home puzzled at Morag's sudden departure. He'd ask her tomorrow why she went so quickly. Now he had to smuggle his wet things into the house without his mother finding out what he'd been up to.

CHAPTER 12

The following day, after delivering the ironing Connor went into the shop to see Danny. He didn't want Danny arranging to meet up with him in the afternoon. The shop was very busy with a few tourists looking at postcards and souvenirs as well as the normal island customers wanting weekend groceries.

Danny grinned when he saw Connor, and carried on serving Colonel Bannister with his small grocery list.

"Dad can I have five minutes with Connor? I won't be too long." His Dad nodded.

"You can have half an hour," he said generously. "You've worked hard this morning lad."

"Thanks." Danny squeezed out from behind the counter, grabbed two cans of coke and manoeuvred his way between the people browsing the shelves. Outside they crossed the road and made their way towards the small harbour.

"Your Dad out fishing?" Danny asked, handing Connor his can. The liquid fizzed and bubbled as he peeled off the lid then he slurped it quickly before it spilled over.

They settled themselves on the harbour wall. The fishing boats of faded red and blue that were still moored, rose and fell on the swelling tide, occasionally rubbing the ancient stone of the harbour, their ropes slapping and cracking against the masts that swayed this way and that.

"He went out early this morning. I hardly ever see him. When he is home he spends his evenings down the pub. I don't know how Mum puts up with it."

"My Mum and Dad are a bit like that, but every now and again Mum has a 'go' and he takes her to the pub with him. Dad plays darts and Mum has a good gossip with Ruby the barmaid... It doesn't happen that often though." They sipped their cokes in silence for a while.

"I won't be able to come today we've got the match remember? You'll be coming to watch won't you?"

Connor had completely forgotten about the match. The last one of the season and really important. His face fell. Danny looked at him surprised.

"You have forgotten. But it makes no difference does it, you're not doing anything special are you?"

Connor didn't know what to say, he was torn in two. He didn't want to let Danny down nor did he want to let Morag down and miss his next swimming lesson. There was an awkward pause.

He forced himself to smile, "Of course I'll be there," he said, "wouldn't miss it for the world." He was rewarded by Danny's beaming grin.

"What did you do yesterday afternoon?"

"I went down onto the beach again. I can manage the steps really well now, as long as I don't hurry. Did you know there's a cave down there?"

"No, are you going to explore it on your own? Oh, wait for me. I'd love to explore a cave."

"Well, I thought I'd have a look, but not go all the way in. I'll have to take a torch."

"I might be able to make it tomorrow. Can you wait till then?"

Connor hesitated, he would want to go swimming with Morag tomorrow if she wasn't too put out by him not turning up today. He wished he hadn't mentioned the cave now.

"There's no rush," Connor replied. "You might be busy in the shop tomorrow. I'll wait till you're sure you can come. We could leave it till Wednesday."

"OK that'll suit me fine. I'd better get back we're really busy. A tourist boat came in this morning and it's been non-stop in the shop, but that's good because Dad pays me. See you this afternoon."

Danny left, and Connor sat on trying to work out how

he was going to tell Morag he couldn't come today. He decided to go to the cove and leave a message somehow. Although he was in a hurry, he knew he knew he mustn't rush in case he fell. It was very frustrating.

He reached the cliff top panting, and rested, taking deep breaths, then carefully navigated the steps. The tide wasn't fully in yet so any message he left had to be above the tide line. He took out his sketch book from his bag and a very soft pencil, and tearing out the last page wrote a note in large black letters.

Sorry, I can't come today.
Hope to see you tomorrow.

Connor signed his name and drew a sad cartoon-type face. He looked around to find a good spot for his note. He wished he could nail it to the cliff face but he couldn't do that. It would have to lie flat, weighed down by stones or else the wind would blow it away. In the end he placed it flat on a large black rock that stood out from the grey rocks around it, beside the steps, high above the tide line. Hopefully she would see the white paper and come to investigate. He sighed deeply and made his way slowly up the steps and home for lunch.

CHAPTER 13

As soon as lunch was over Connor set off for the football pitch. He limped along, overtaken by the families that were on their way to support their lads who were playing that day. Danny's Mum caught him up and walked with him for a while asking after his Mum and Dad and talking non-stop about how useful Danny was in the shop now that he was older.

"I'll go ahead now Connor. Shall I keep you a place by me?"

"Thank you Mrs Stewart that would be great."

When Connor arrived, the rails around the pitch were full of enthusiastic supporters from both sides. He studied the crowd and soon saw Mrs Stewart. He pushed his way through the press of people to join her. Mrs Stewart smiled and budged up a bit more to make room for him. To Connor's dismay he realised too late that Moira was on the other side of her. Of course she would be here cheering on her boyfriend. Why didn't he think of that? Connor sighed determined to ignore any barbed comments she might send his way.

Mr Baxter was there surrounded by the team dressed in the school colours of blue and gold. He was obviously giving them tactical advice. They were all listening intently to him. Then the whistle blew and both teams dispersed to their places on the field.

Connor could not concentrate on the game. Having never played it and not having a television where he could watch matches, he really wasn't interested. His mind kept drifting to the cove and wondering if Morag had got his message and wondering what her reaction would be. The roar of the crowd brought him back from his wondering. Someone had scored a goal, but he wasn't sure who till he saw the excited faces of Mrs Stewart and Moira. He joined in the cheering then, but not before Moira had noticed how slow he had been to respond.

At half time the score was two one to The Island Academy. Danny's team leading. He looked up at them and waved before drinking down a whole bottle of water. Moira was blowing him kisses with her hand. Connor had to look away, embarrassed at the exhibition.

The game continued with both Rory and Danny racing about the field. They seemed to be everywhere at once. Then the opposing team scored so it was a draw. Everybody was screaming encouragement now as the minutes were ticking away and both sides were determined to win, but then Ewan passed the ball to Danny who passed it to Rory who neatly kicked it between the goal posts. The whistle blew. The Island Academy had won! The supporters erupted with jubilant shouts, whistles and cheers. The sound was deafening.

The players all shook hands or clapped each other on the back then stood in a row while the presentations were made. The losing team were given certificates and everyone clapped and cheered as they had done well to get this far. The winners were each presented with a medallion commemorating the event and the captain was presented with a huge silver cup which would be displayed at school. The boys were all very pleased with themselves and did a circuit of the field holding the cup high for everyone to admire.

Mrs Stewart, Connor and Moira waited for Danny so they could all walk home together.

"You must come back for a celebration to our house. Danny will be so excited," said Mrs Stewart.

As soon as Danny appeared Moira flew to him and gave him a huge hug. Danny went bright red and just managed to disentangle himself, so he could hug his Mum. He grinned at Connor.

"Glad you could make it. It was a great game wasn't it?"

"Fat lot of attention Connor was paying; he was gazing into the distance for most of the match," Moira chipped in spitefully.

It was Connor's turn to blush. "That was just the beginning," he defended himself.

"Well anyway," said Mrs Stewart, "let's get on I've made a large chocolate cake and cans of fizzy drinks from the shop." She frowned at Moira, who didn't seem to notice.

Connor did his best to keep up but in the end made an excuse to say he had an errand to do for his Mum and he'd join them in a bit.

"Thank goodness for that," he heard Moira say as he watched them walk ahead.

Connor turned into a side street that twisted its way down towards the harbour. He didn't stop, but once at the harbour turned up the street that would bring him out near Danny's shop. He walked to the house door behind the shop and rang the bell. Mr Stewart came and ushered him inside.

Danny was sitting on the sofa with Moira and talking loudly about the match, going over every detail.

"Hi Connor have some cake," he said as soon as Connor walked in.

"What would you like to drink Connor?" Mr Stewart indicated the heavily laden table.

"Just a coke please," he answered. Mrs Stewart bustled in from the kitchen and cut Connor a large piece of cake handing it to him on a plate.

"Did you get your errand done?"

"Yes, thank you."

"It's good the way you're helping your Mum Connor."
Mr Stewart interrupted at this point.

"I think we should toast our school team now and the amazing victory! Hopefully you'll repeat it next year," he added looking at Danny.

They all drank to the success of the team, then Mrs Stewart went into the kitchen to prepare the evening meal and Mr Stewart into the other room to read the paper and put his feet up after a busy day.

"D'you remember the first goal we got Connor? The way Iain booted it in?" Moira said turning to him.

"Yes, I think so," he hesitated. Moira burst out laughing, Danny looked a bit puzzled.

"Iain didn't score the first goal. It was Danny! I told you he wasn't watching," Moira hooted. "Connor you're priceless! Fancy not noticing Danny scoring the first goal!"

"Didn't you follow the match?" Danny asked looking a bit disappointed and frowning slightly.

"I had something on my mind, just at the start, I followed it after that."

"I could tell you didn't want to come when I reminded you. You didn't even remember! The match of the season! Not even interested in your best friend's game, and I've helped you so much over the last week." He was angrier than Connor had ever seen him.

Connor felt wretched. It was true, he wasn't interested in football and he also knew that Danny had been there for him all the time, encouraging him and helping him to become more confident and it couldn't have been much fun for him, but he still did it.

Connor got to his feet. "I'm really sorry Danny. You have been the best friend anyone could have, and you deserved better from me." He left as quick as he could, stumbling in the hall way. He didn't want anyone to see the tears that were brimming and threatening to spill down his cheeks.

CHAPTER 14

Connor didn't want to go home until he'd fully calmed down. Not wanting his Mum to suspect anything. There was only one place he could go to be sure of not meeting anyone… the cliff top.

A cold wind had whipped in from the north. Grey clouds bunched together across the sky and spread like a slatey roof over the island. The sea streaked with white caps, choppy and frothy, foamed around the headlands and sent dazzling white fountains over the rocks and up the cliff face. The sea roared, the wind howled, the gulls screamed. Connor's ears rang with the noise, numb with the cold, his heart echoed the wild and turbulent elements. All his joy and happiness had evaporated in one afternoon.

He flung himself down on the grass and rolled over onto his back staring up at the sky. The clouds strode across the heavens at such a pace that Connor, for a moment, thought he was moving and the clouds were still. It was a very odd sensation.

He hated Moira and thumped the grass with his fists. Why was she so spiteful? She deliberately watched him, to catch him out. The awful thing was it was true, he hadn't watched the match at the beginning, and he hadn't really wanted to be there at all. He'd only gone because of Danny. Well, she had Danny to herself now. Connor couldn't believe he'd lost the only real friend he had. The tears brimmed over and he scrubbed at his eyes angrily. Morag probably wouldn't want to know him now either because he hadn't turned up as he promised. He closed his eyes and just lay there on the grass listening to the wind, the sea and the gulls and his own heart thumping away in his chest as if nothing had happened.

After a while he sat up and gazed out to sea. A lone fishing boat was making its way slowly towards the harbour, buffeted by the wind and pounded by the waves.

63

It sometimes disappeared completely as it dipped down into a trough between the waves only to see it reappear on the crest of the next wave. But it was slowly and bravely drawing nearer to the quayside and the relative peace of the harbour.

Watching the struggles of the little fishing boat, produced a calm in Connor's soul. It seemed to be a picture of what he was going through, fighting his way through seemingly insurmountable difficulties to reach some sort of peace.

The words of Mr Hughes came back to him and his courage returned. No matter what happened he was going to follow his dream of college or university. He didn't know how he was to achieve this, but he was resolved to give it his best shot, even without the help of friends and family. He gave his face a final rub to remove any traces of tears and made his way home for his tea.

***

The next afternoon Connor arrived early again, his heart thudding in his chest and a tight feeling in his throat, hoping and praying that Morag would come and not be too angry with him for letting her down. The tide was still washing the lower steps so he sat and waited watching the waves slap and crack against the base of the cliff. Sea birds were screaming and squabbling, soaring up on taut outspread wings. There were plenty of nests on the rocky ledges of the cliffs. Most of the young birds had fledged but they still returned to the ledges to rest after flying about over the ocean searching for food. They made such a racket, sometimes dive-bombing each other or chasing after each other to steal food. Connor did a few lightning sketches and, as he was looking at the cliffs, didn't see Morag emerging from the waves dragging her big cloak behind her. She flung it in a heap on an outcrop of rocks high above sea level before calling to Connor.

"Where were you yesterday? I waited and waited, but you didn't come. Don't you want to learn to swim anymore?" Connor turned, his heart missing a beat. Glad that she'd come but wondering how she would be towards him.

"Didn't you get my note?" he asked, his voice shaking slightly.

"D'you mean this?" She produced a mangled, dripping piece of paper from somewhere about her person and waved it in the air.

"I didn't understand it," she said, letting it go, as the wind tugged it from her hand. It spiralled up before landing on the sea like a square, white bird.

"I couldn't make it. I'd promised my friend to go to a football match. I'd forgotten all about it." Morag stared at him for a long while in silence. Connor sighed. "I didn't really want to go. I wanted to come here. But he's a good friend and I had promised... but forgot."

"Do you still want to learn to swim… properly, strongly?"

"Yes I do. I love it!" There was a pause.

"You'd better change then and come in." She turned and running out into deeper water dived expertly through the waves.

Connor shut his book and stuffed it into his bag before quickly changing into his trunks. He very carefully and slowly made his way down the slope, which had once been steps, hanging onto the cliff wall.

When he reached the sea Morag was there holding out her hands to steady him. They didn't have to wade far as the water became deep very quickly and soon Connor's feet left the sandy shore and he was kicking his legs and moving forward, with Morag's help, through the water.

The joy surged up in him again. What a wonderful

feeling of freedom.

"You have to use your arms now. You can paddle them back and fore like this." Connor copied what she did and found himself moving forwards slowly. "Or do this." Her arms moved like windmill sails curving powerfully through the water. Once more Connor copied, turning his head from side to side as he'd seen her do.

This was much better, he moved swiftly through the water, Morag racing beside him.

"Are you sure you've never swum before?" She asked.

He dog-paddled for a bit to catch his breath. "No never, but I have watched swimmers on my friend's television and seen how they do it." Connor swam back and fore, Morag shouting instructions to help him perfect his stroke.

"D'you want to try floating. It's great, just lying on the sea staring at the sky?"

"I'll give it a go."

Morag demonstrated. "Just lie back like this, give yourself to the sea, let her hold you, rest on her."

Connor turned onto his back, but buckled in the middle and began to sink.

"No," said Morag holding him up while he spluttered. "Put your head back and lie flat. That's right. How does it feel?"

"Wonderful," Connor murmured. "I could go to sleep."

"Well don't. We have to keep practising actual swimming. You can rest like that when you're tired. Come on, let's swim to that rock," she said pointing to a rock halfway to the headland sticking out of the sea like a broken tooth.

Connor turned onto his front and struck out towards the rock. By the time he was half-way there he had to stop and float. Morag swam back to him.

"Have you enough energy to swim back?"

"Oh yes. Next time I'm going to reach the rock." They swam leisurely towards the shore. Connor's legs were shaking with the effort he had made by the time they reached the sand. He flopped down lying back with his eyes closed his chest heaving. Morag sat quietly beside him, watching.

"You'll be a strong swimmer one day," she said. Connor opened his eyes and turned his head to look at her.

"D'you think so?" He half smiled.

"I know so," she said.

CHAPTER 15

"Haven't seen Danny with you since the match on Saturday." Connor's mother remarked on Monday morning, as she swished the iron back and fore across the crisp white sheets. "Spending all his time with that girl Moira no doubt. I'm surprised though, you and Danny always got on so well together."

Connor just grunted his reply not wanting to go over the painful details with his mother. "Shall I do some deliveries for you this morning?" he offered, changing the subject. "People have been giving me tips Mum. Is it alright if I keep them and save them up? I'll need a new sketch book soon and they're quite expensive."

His mother stood the iron up on the board and looked at him, then began to fold the sheet carefully.

"I'm grateful to you for saving my time, so anything they give you, you can keep as far as I'm concerned. Don't tell your Dad what you want to spend it on though. He wouldn't understand."

That morning Connor earned another two pounds. He avoided Danny's grocery shop, passing by on the other side of the street, his heart heavy, wishing they could be friends again.

***

Morag was waiting for him when he arrived at the cove, sitting on a rock and throwing pebbles into the swirling waves. She turned when she heard Connor coming down the steps and gave him a cheerful grin.

"Are we racing to the rock today?"

"Can't wait," Connor replied sitting down toeing off his trainers and peeling off his jeans and tee shirt. The wind was chilly and brought goose-bumps out on

Connor's arms.

The pair walked slowly down the slope and slid into the water, which was quite deep as the tide was fully in. They were soon swimming side by side and diving through the waves. Morag was able to stay under water far longer than Connor, but Connor practised, taking deeper breaths to increase his lung capacity.

After just messing about for a bit they set off for the rock. Morag keeping closely beside him the further they swum from the land. As they neared the rock she shouted encouragement to Connor as she could see he was beginning to flag, but they reached the rock. Morag climbed up first then leant down and helped Connor. His chest was heaving; he was blowing out long breaths as he climbed up beside her.

"Whoo! That was fantastic! I never thought I'd do it." He slicked his hair back from his face, panting, and stared at the distant cove which appeared so tiny. It almost disappeared, swallowed up by the surrounding craggy cliffs. The rock itself was much bigger than Connor had expected, parts of it covered in bird poo, especially the middle where the sea seldom reached except in a storm.

"We'll have a good rest here," Morag said, "before we set off back."

"Did it take you long to learn to swim?" Connor asked Morag. "I feel as if I've been swimming all my life now."

"We learn to swim as soon as we're born."

Connor gaped at her. "Your Mum and Dad took you in the sea... when you were a baby?"

"It's the best time to learn." She leant back closing her eyes, basking in the sun.

"Have you got a big family?" Connor asked really curious about this strange girl.

"I have two older brothers, and two younger sisters."

"Do you all live together?"

"Of course."

69

"But where Morag… on another island… or the mainland?"

"Another island Connor. I'll tell you about it one day. What about you? Tell me about your friend Danny and the football match?" Connor frowned.

"We fell out about that. It was a good match, Danny played well, but I wasn't concentrating properly on it, and his girlfriend, Moira, pointed this out to him and he got really angry… so that's it."

"That's it?" Morag sat up and stared at him in horror. "He can't be much of a friend if he quarrelled with you just because you didn't… watch him… perform… in this game!"

"No, he was a very good friend. None of the others, maybe Rory, sometimes, ever wanted to spend time with me because I couldn't join in with their games. Danny was always there for me."

"In that case I'm sure you'll be friends again." She relaxed back on the rock closing her eyes.

They stayed on the rock a while longer enjoying the warmth of the sun. The wind had dropped slightly and the sea was smooth as glass.

"Ready to go back?" Morag asked.

"Yep."

"I'll show you how to dive. It's safe here, no hidden rocks." She stood, lifted her arms above her head and dived neatly into the sea, bobbing up again a few feet away. Climbing back onto the rock she showed Connor how to stand. It was awkward for him with uneven legs, but he stood balancing his right leg on its toes. He quite often did this when he needed to and it worked. He took a deep breath and leant forward. He made an enormous splash as his belly contacted the water first. He came up laughing.

"I don't think that went according to plan!"

Morag dived in beside him. "We'll have to practise some more. Back to the cove now!" They struck out for

70

the shore.

The tide had receded leaving a stretch of untouched sand, like a blank page waiting to be written on. Connor walked over to the steps and dried himself and dressed before joining Morag on the sand. She was making patterns with a stick. At first Connor thought she was writing as the patterns were in a long straight line.

"I thought for a minute you were writing," he said when he joined her.

"This is my writing," she replied.

"What does it say?"

"It doesn't talk Connor."

"But…" he stopped. "You can't read or write can you. That's why my note didn't mean anything to you. Don't you go to school?"

"I don't really know what school is."

Connor was totally mystified. "A place where kids go to learn things?"

"We learn everything we need at home."

The light dawned!

"You're Home Schooled!" He knew lots of children living in remote areas were taught at home. Some had computers and others received their work in the post. "I don't know that I'd like that, in spite of everything it's good to meet up with others, great fun on occasions." But that still didn't explain why she couldn't read or write. Maybe she was dyslexic.

"I could teach you if you want. You're teaching me to swim. I'll teach you to read and write."

Morag smiled, her eyes dancing. "Then we could send messages to each other."

Connor set to work drawing the letters of her name in the sand.

"This is your name M, O, R, A, G. Now you copy it underneath." She took the stick from him and copied her name in wobbly letters.

"Good. Now this is my name. He wrote C, O, N, N, O, R. Your turn." He handed her the stick. They continued like this till the beach was covered with random words and Connor realised it was time he left for his evening meal, and then he remembered.

"I won't be able to come tomorrow I'm going to the Big House to study paintings. I could write some words down for you to practise if you like and we'll meet up again on Wednesday afternoon?"

Morag didn't look too happy about it. "I suppose so," She sighed.

Connor tore a page from his sketch book and carefully wrote their names in big letters, then chose several words related to swimming that he'd already written in the sand. Morag was very pleased.

"I'll hide it high up in the cave so it won't get wet," she said turning away and heading for the base of the cliffs.

"Where is the cave?" Connor called after her.

"I'll show you another day. Goodbye!" And she disappeared, melting into the rocks.

Connor shook his head in bewilderment and gathered up his belongings, stuffed his towel and swimming trunks into his bag, turned towards the steps, and home.

CHAPTER 16

Heavy clouds had rolled in overnight sending sharp spatters of rain against the window pane. Connor woke with a start. The sea heaving and pitching leaden shoulders that frothed with breakers. It was gloomy in the cottage and the kitchen light was on when he arrived downstairs for breakfast.

"Dad's not going out in this is he?" Connor asked his Mum. A worried frown formed dark creases across her forehead.

"You know your Dad. He's gone already." She sighed. "D'you think you can manage to deliver these?" she indicated the pile on the dresser with a flick of her head. "Without being blown over."

Connor pulled a face. "No problem. I'm getting stronger all the time. Haven't you noticed?"

"Well you look a lot healthier. Your legs and arms are quite brown and you're filling out a bit. The fresh air's doing you good, but I don't want you to overdo it and set yourself back." Connor grinned to himself if only she knew, he thought.

It took him all morning to deliver the ironing and by lunchtime the massive purple clouds had blown away and a sky the delicate blue of a thrush's egg, arched over the island. The wind was still quite brisk though. He rushed his lunch desperate to reach the Big House and maybe have the chance to draw some of the wild flowers in their garden as well as looking through the Art books.

"You're in a tearing hurry today. Going somewhere special?" his Mum asked.

He shook his head, hopefully not looking too guilty.

"Just out." he replied grabbing his bag and making for the door.

He knew he was going to arrive too early so he slowed his pace and took the long way round, past the harbour.

73

The sea was still heaving and pitching, slapping the quay side with pistol-shot waves, the spray spewing over onto the pavement before running back down in rivulets into the harbour. The sun sparkled and glittered in the pools. Overhead the gulls glided and soared, wings motionless, borne up on unseen currents of air, now and again diving down squabbling and screaming over a tasty crab or starfish stranded on the quayside by a receding wave. The tumult engulfed Connor, making him feel quite giddy and he was glad to turn into a side street that would eventually lead him to the Big House. As soon as Connor turned away from the harbour the hubbub diminished as if someone had flicked a switch.

He liked this street. The houses had small front gardens that were tended carefully by the residents. Hollyhocks swayed in the wind beside the windows, in front of the climbing roses that scrambled over doorways and small stone porches. The fuchsia hedges were in bud, some already bursting from their green sheaths and hanging like noiseless ruby bells that swung to and fro. Silver leafed lavender thrust stiff purple spikes through the railings, and bright geraniums decorated the window boxes.

Connor re-joined the main street, eventually reaching the drive that led to the Big House. He was still a bit early but hoped it wouldn't matter too much. He rang the bell and waited, gazing at the flower borders that edged the drive. They were very neat and orderly, nothing like the wild abandonment of the garden at the back of the house.

The door opened and a tall woman stood framed in the doorway. The first thing that Connor noticed was that her eyes were a cool, pale grey, that were startlingly bright against her tanned skin. Her blue-black hair tumbled around her shoulders in curls and waves but gleamed like satin. She wore a pair of paint spattered jeans and a loose tee shirt also streaked with paint.

She smiled then and tucking a strand of hair behind her

74

ear said, "You must be Connor. Come in. Thomas has told me a lot about you." Connor followed this amazing-looking woman into the library. Mr Hughes was standing at the table arranging open books across its wide shiny surface.

He looked up. "Ah Connor, good to see you. This is my wife Sasha." He smiled a warm welcoming smile. Mrs Hughes walked over to the table glancing at the books that were spread out.

"Can I see your sketches Connor?" she asked.

Connor joined them at the table and fumbled in his bag for his sketch book and held it out to her. He was tongue-tied in their presence. She studied each page her eyes resting longer on the drawings of flowers and birds.

"Oh Thomas," she cried, "you can't keep him cooped up in here looking at other people's work. These drawings are wonderful! He needs to be out in the garden drawing our flowers."

Mr Hughes gave a gentle chuckle. "I suppose you're right, as always Sasha." and looking up at Connor he asked. "Would you like to join my wife in the garden? There's a sheltered spot you can sit in out of the wind, although it does seem to have dropped a bit."

Connor's face broke into a dazzling smile. "I'd love to." he replied.

"Follow me then Connor," she moved at a brisk pace, then slowed as she reached the French windows realising that Connor couldn't keep up. They walked out into the sunshine together, Sasha asking questions and Connor answering them as best he could.

The garden stretched out before them; the grass knee-deep waving feathery plumes, Ox-eye daisies in tall snow-white clumps among a scattering of golden buttercups, and purple spikes of thistles.

The long grass dragged against Connor's legs as they made their way towards the sheltered spot Mr Hughes had mentioned. Heady scents rose in a fragrant cloud and the comfortable hum of bees provided a musical background.

An easel had been set up next to a wooden bench in a curve of shrubs and bushes. The air was still in this place. Connor was curious to see what Mrs Hughes had been drawing.

"Well, what do you think?" She said, turning the easel towards him. "I've decided to try my hand at fabric design."

A large piece of paper was tacked to a drawing board on the easel and was covered with stylised drawings of various plants, leaves and flowers. Connor could name everyone, but it was almost as if she had redesigned each of them to form a shape or a pattern.

"I like them," he began hesitatingly. "I can see you're adapting them for something else. Are you going to paint them?"

"Eventually, I thought I'd just get as much down as I could and later choose which ones work together. Now what about you?"

Connor took a deep breath. "I just want to draw them as they are," he said, his face shining with delight.

"That's a good starting point. Do you want to sit on the bench?"

"I'd like to be out there among them all," he replied gesturing with his hand, embracing the whole garden.

"That's OK by me. We'll stop for tea at half past three and see how you've got on."

Connor roamed through the long grass careful to not trample any of the flowers. Then settled himself down to draw a bunch of Ox-eye daisies. He was soon lost in his own world, moving from flower to flower and drawing swathes of plumy grasses. He was startled when Sasha called him for tea. They walked together to the house, Connor chatting more readily about the loveliness of the garden.

76

Once inside, and tea and lemonade poured, the couple examined Connor's work. They were fascinated to hear that he'd had no tuition from anyone or even encouragement from his parents.

"These are so full of life Connor!" Mrs Hughes exclaimed. "And in this one, of the grasses, you've caught the wind blowing through it. It's lovely." Connor blushed, not knowing what to say.

"You've definitely got a future young man, if you're prepared to take it," Mr Hughes said admiring Connor's work. "Look at this," he said, turning the book towards his wife. It was the page of his drawings of Morag. "Who's the girl?"

"Where did you learn to draw people like that? She's so lively, exuberant! I can see you prefer flowers, but your drawings of people are excellent, the fishermen, the harbour, the boats. They're all so good."

"I don't think you'd have any trouble getting into a college on the mainland… You don't look very keen." Mr Hughes was frowning in a puzzled way.

"It's not that. I'd love to go to college, but I don't think my Dad would let me go." Mr Hughes sighed and he and his wife exchanged glances. "We'll cross that bridge when we come to it. Meanwhile would you like my wife to teach you a bit, different techniques and things like that, to open up your talent?"

"I'd love that more than anything," Connor answered, his eyes shining.

"OK, let's start now," said Mrs Hughes rising to her feet and heading for the open French windows.

CHAPTER 17

Connor walked home in a daze, his feet hardly touching the pavement, his head buzzing with thoughts of a bright future and feeling that he was a person in his own right. Not a victim of a disability, but a whole being, knowing that two people believed in him and were prepared to help him achieve his goal. Because that's what they had given him, a goal and a future.

"You look very pleased with yourself," his mother remarked when he walked in. "Drawing again, I suppose."

"Yes Mum. I've done some good drawings today and I've made up my mind to try to get into an Art College on the main land, after I've done my exams of course."

"And what d'you think your father's going to say about that?"

"I don't care anymore, he sees me as a useless person, and I don't think he'll ever see me any different, so there's no point me trying to please him, it'll never happen, so I might as well do what I want."

There was an uneasy silence as they sat to eat their meal.

"Have you seen anything of Danny?"

Connor shook his head and stared down at his plate.

"What happened between you two? you've been friends since infant school. Is it that girl? I never liked her."

Connor explained briefly what had happened. "I should have taken more notice of the game, but she needn't have pointed it out to Danny. It was only the beginning of the match I missed."

"What were you thinking about to make you so distracted?"

"Oh just… things," Connor shrugged thinking guiltily about his secret friendship with Morag. Then, changing the subject hurriedly, "Would you like me to deliver those tonight?" he asked indicating with a nod of his head the neat pile of ironed garments on the sideboard.

"Well that would save you tomorrow, although there'll be more."

After tea Mrs McKenzie put the laundry into bags and handed them to Connor.

"This one is for the Mermaid pub at the top of the High Street, and this one for the Rosemount Bed and Breakfast in Harbour Road. Can you manage both bags?"

Connor nodded and set off into the calm evening air. The sun was leaning towards the west and shadows were lengthening. There was no wind now. Peace inside and out he thought and I'm glad I told Mum about my plans.

He delivered the laundry and received some money to add to his savings, then walked on over the headland to the sandy bay on the other side.

There were holiday cottages here and the beach was private, so Connor had rarely visited it with Danny. The road wound its way along the top, flanked by low scrubby bushes of heather and broom. Where the road dipped down, it ran through a long stand of stunted trees twisted by the wind into tormented shapes. Connor hadn't brought his sketch book but decided he would definitely return to draw these twisted trees.

***

Morag was drawing in the sand when Connor arrived the following afternoon. He walked over to her. She held the piece of paper in her left hand and was copying the letters in big shaky shapes with a stick in her right hand. Her teeth were gritted together and her forehead creased with a frown as she concentrated.

"That's very good," Connor exclaimed. "They're quite recognisable. I can see that's your name."

"It's much harder than it looks," she said, not looking

79

up. "The stick doesn't want to go where I want to put it."

"You're going to have to use a shorter stick. You'll have more control then." Connor looked around at the tide line where driftwood, shells and seaweed were strewn where the tide had abandoned them. He broke off a bleached twig from a tree branch that lay adorned with seaweed and brought it to Morag.

"Here, try this," he said. She looked up and took it from him and began to trace out huge letters once more.

"No, no not like that. You need to do them smaller now, more like my writing." He took the twig and showed her how to form the smaller letters, then handed it back.

"That's better," she smiled looking at her handiwork with pride. "I can make it do what I like now it's smaller."

"Are we going swimming?" Connor asked.

"Of course." She jumped up brushing the sand from her hands, and handed him the piece of paper with the words that he had written out for her. "Can you look after that while we swim?"

Connor took it and put it in his bag, stripped off his tee shirt and jeans and began to hobble to the edge of the sea with Morag.

"I think the sea should be rougher don't you? More of a challenge?"

Connor shot her a surprised look, but her eyes were closed and she was muttering again. He looked back at the sea and the waves indeed were rising and crashing onto the beach much wilder than before.

"Did you do that?" His voice high with amazement.

She just gave him a wicked grin and slipped beneath the oncoming wave which took Connor by surprise and knocked him over. He surfaced laughing and spluttering as another wave smacked him in the face. He began to swim after her rising with the swell, feeling the tug of the current pulling him into the curving water towering above him, pushing through into the trough between the waves, always moving steadily forward, but not catching her up.

It was more tiring swimming in such boisterous waters and soon Connor floated on his back, once he'd passed the huge waves and was in choppy water that lifted him and dropped him as if he was a cork or a piece of flotsam. Morag joined him.

"Have you had enough? It's good to practise in all sorts of sea. It makes you stronger."

"Yeah I can believe that," Connor panted.

"We ought to swim to the rock again. D'you think you can?"

Connor rolled onto his front and struck out for the rock in answer to her question. They reached and clambered up, Connor's chest heaving with the exertion.

"You're getting really good at this," Morag laughed, "you'll soon be a champion swimmer, beating all your friends."

The sun decided to appear from behind the clouds and shone down upon them with a fierce heat that was very welcome. Connor could feel it burning his arms and shoulders, as he sat relaxing in its warmth.

He lay back, shutting his eyes. "Did you honestly make the sea choppier?" He murmured sleepily not wanting to open his eyes, enjoying resting in the sunshine.

"What do you think?" Morag replied dreamily. Connor sat up again.

"I don't know what to think. You haven't actually told me much about yourself." Morag turned on her side, propped her chin on her hand and looked up at him.

"Mmm, maybe I'll trust you." Then rising to her feet cried "Race you to the beach!" and dived into the water swimming strongly for the shore. Connor followed, performing a spectacular belly-flop, (he hadn't perfected diving yet,) before racing after her.

CHAPTER 18

To Morag's surprise they reached the beach together.

"You caught me up! You really are getting to be a strong swimmer."

"I've had a good teacher," Connor replied flopping down beside his bag and reaching for his towel. "I need to practise diving though. Belly-flopping's not much fun." Morag laughed.

"Can you write me some more words?"

Connor pulled out the paper and taking a pencil wrote down a list of objects to do with the beach and the sea; shell, wave, stick, cliff, cave, swimming, diving. "Will that do? I'll bring you a notebook and a pen next time, then you can practise all you like."

"I'll keep them in the cave. Would you like to see it now?"

"It'll be pitch black. We won't be able to see a thing. I could bring a torch next time if you like."

"A torch?"

"You know… a light so we can see where we're going."

"Oh a torch, we won't need that, the rocks are phosphorescent."

Connor frowned. He didn't really like the idea of dark caves. He wanted to sit in the fresh air and sunshine. But it was obvious Morag was determined.

"OK then wait till I'm dressed." Morag wandered off to scratch the new words in the sand. When he was ready he called to her and she led the way around an outcrop of rocks. Connor followed reluctantly.

"Morag, I really don't fancy a dark slimy cave."

She took no notice of his moaning. "You'll love this it's not dark, it's beautiful."

Connor sighed and saw, a tall narrow cleft in the cliff face. Morag disappeared inside humming to herself:

Rocks of crystal make me a light
Shine your jewels into the night.
Twinkle and sparkle like stars, moon and sun
And light up the darkness as if day had begun.

Whether it was a trick of the sunlight filtering down from a hole in the roof and reflecting from the many pools, Connor didn't know, but a soft glow was emanating from the cleft as he moved carefully forward over the slippery rocks. As he drew nearer, the glow brightened until he was walking into a space lit up like day by the glowing walls of the cave.

Morag was standing in the centre on a large flat rock turning slowly around, arms out-spread gazing at the sparkling walls that surrounded her.

"Do you like it?" she asked. Her face shining as the cave itself.

"Like it? It's amazing! I've never seen anything like this. You did it didn't you? That song you were singing about stars and stuff. Who are you?"

"Haven't you guessed yet Connor? I'm a Selkie!" For a moment the cave seemed to turn upside down. Connor put out a hand to steady himself against the cave wall.

"Say that again. A Selkie?" Then "Oh I get it," he gave a shaky laugh. "You're having me on… the swimming and stuff. You know the legend as well as I do."

"You don't want to believe me do you?" Morag said marching angrily down the slope towards him. "You'd rather stay in the darkness of ignorance." She punched down with her hand and all the beautiful lights went out. The cave was filled with inky blackness. Connor yelped.

"Morag. Please put the lights back on again." He

83

begged, his voice high with fright. He couldn't see his hand in front of his face and he wasn't at all sure which way to turn to leave the cave.

"Not so sure now, are you human boy?" her voice was very close, he hadn't heard her move to his side. Then he felt the air stir as she moved away again. A soft glow began to creep up the walls once more, enabling Connor to see her again. She was standing, hands on hips, glaring down at Connor. She did indeed look like a royal princess. He heard her sigh, and watched as she sank down on the rock, elbows on knees, chin propped in her hands. She looked dejected and defeated, staring blankly at the rocky floor of the cave.

Connor struggled clumsily over the rocks and slumped down beside her. He didn't know what to say, his thoughts in turmoil. So decided on the truth.

"I never expected to meet a real live Selkie. We've all been brought up to believe that they are creatures of legend. But I did wonder about you, the way you appeared, without a boat, and not living or staying on the island. Where do you come from?"

"Sule Skerry." She lifted her head and her huge brown eyes looked at him full of tremendous sadness.

"That's miles away," Connor exclaimed.

"I know, but sometimes my family swim this way following the eels and I sneak here to play on the land. I love to have legs and run and skip and dance. I'd seen you, with your friend on the steps. I wanted to meet you. I wanted a human friend to run with." She hesitated. "When I saw you walking on the sand I knew you wouldn't be able to run with me, but then I thought I could share the freedom of the sea with you. You could swim and dive with me and be my friend."

Connor tried to take all this in. "Haven't you got any friends of your own?"

"Yes, but they don't want legs. They're quite happy to

84

remain in the sea. And my full name and title is Morag Senga Lachina which translated means Princess Purity of the Land of the Lochs, and it's simply not done for a princess to walk on land and befriend humans."

"But you want to."

"I just wanted to find out what all the fuss was about."

"You've lost me. What fuss?"

"The Selkies hate humans, and have done for centuries. In the past Selkies have been captured as something to be put on show and stared at. Of course the captured ones invariably died longing for the sea and their families, their cloaks taken from them and only returned for them to transform and swim round a tank. Then, once that's over the cloaks are taken away again till the next performance."

"So that's what your cloak is all about! But Morag that doesn't happen now. No-one has ever seen a Selkie. We just think they are a legend … a story!"

"That may be true but the hatred goes on. Seals and Selkies alike have been shot and killed now, because of the fish."

"What about the fish?"

"Humans believe the seals attack the fish farms, but we prefer eels to salmon, but they still come and shoot us with their guns."

"But that's seals, not Selkies!"

"Oh dear, Connor, d'you think they can tell the difference? Would they even stop to think? Several of our closest relatives were destroyed in the last cull and those that survived are bent on revenge."

Connor had heard about seal culling and thought it was cruel and shouldn't be done.

"I'm so sorry Morag. I know some people are trying to stop it."

"I hope they do Connor. I really hope they do."

It was beginning to get very cold in the cave and Connor's teeth were chattering.

"Can we go back out into the sunshine? It's freezing in here."

Morag increased the brightness and leant Connor her arm to steady him over the pebbly floor. As they walked out onto the sand, the cave returned to deepest darkness.

CHAPTER 19

The heat hit them like opening an oven door. It had been the hottest Summer for several years. Connor soon warmed up.

"Tell me more about the cloaks. You mentioned cloaks. How do they work?"

Morag stooped and picked up the garment that always accompanied her. She spread it wide between her hands and Connor could see it wasn't a heavy coat, it was a voluminous cloak that could wrap right round a body.

"This is what enables me to change into a Selkie. When I take it off, I'm a human like you, with legs and arms. Do you want to try it?"

Connor's eyes flew wide. "D'you mean it would work on me?"

Morag nodded. "As long as the clasp is fastened."

"Wow that's really scary!"

"Scary?" Morag frowned, puzzled.

"Well amazing! I mean." Connor added.

"Come on Connor give it a try. You'll love it!"

"I'll have to change back into my swimming trunks."

Morag shrugged and waited patiently.

When he was ready they walked down to the sea, Morag holding the cloak. When the water reached their waists she handed the cloak to Connor and helped him drape it over his shoulders.

"Now fasten the clasp," she commanded.

As soon as the clasp was fastened, Connor tingled from head to toe. His arms began to shrink and flatten into flippers, his body swelled and ballooned, spreading down his legs until it reached his feet which flattened and transformed into matching flippers. His eyes became huge and his ears disappeared. The wonderful thing was he could swim under the water. His sleek body sliced through the waves like a torpedo. Morag soon joined him, racing and diving, though Morag had to rise to the surface for air more often. Eventually she signalled for him to turn for the shore, the cloak unclasped itself and Connor found he was floundering in deep water, arms and legs flailing about as panic set in.

Morag grabbed his arms and pulled him to the surface. The cloak had tangled round his legs. He swallowed large amounts of salty water before gulping in the air, when they reached the surface. Morag untangled his legs and he felt firm sand beneath his feet. They staggered up the beach together both laughing now at the mad scramble to get him to safety.

They threw themselves down on the sand soaking up the warmth of the sun.

"I can't believe that just happened!" Connor exclaimed. "I was a seal! How amazing is that!" He sat up. "I'd love to do it again."

"Maybe next time. You need to learn how to swim under water and practise diving... which you're very bad at." Connor reached for a strand of seaweed and flicked it at her. She grabbed it and they tussled over it, rolling across the sand laughing.

"Now you have to teach me some more words," she threatened leaning over him and dangling the seaweed a bit above his face.

"OK, OK I surrender!" They stood and walked back up the beach where the sand was drier but still firm, and Connor explained about pronouns 'I' and 'You', nouns and verbs, scratching them in the sand. Morag copied, repeating each word as she went. Then Connor wrote short sentences which Morag copied and repeated aloud.

"Now, you make up a sentence," Connor suggested, "using the words you've just written." Morag studied the words then wrote:

'I like sand.' and then 'I like Connor.'

The last sentence startled Connor and colour rose in

his cheeks. No girl had ever admitted to liking him, though he was friendly with several in his class at school.

"That's very good," he acknowledged gruffly. Then set about explaining the word 'the' that accompanied most common nouns. Morag wrote a new sentence.

'I like the sea'

"That's right. You've got it. All you need to do now is practise."

"Like you and diving," she asserted. "But, I can't come tomorrow Connor. We're having a family get-together. But you could still practise your diving."

He nodded, "You're a hard task master. I'll walk over to Gaelcreags and get a notebook and pen for you. Can we meet up the next afternoon?"

"Of course, I'll be here and we can practise diving."

"I'd better get dressed and go home." He was very sandy and had to brush the dry sand from his legs and arms before scrambling into his clothes. "See you the day after tomorrow," Connor sais making for the steps walking on 'cloud nine'.

***

A frosty silence greeted him when he arrived home for his tea. His elation over the marvellous experience of swimming as a seal evaporated, and his heart which had been singing with happiness, became lead in his chest. Connor was puzzled. His Mum had been fine with him that morning.

She put his meal before him, her mouth in a tight line.

"Thanks Mum," Connor mumbled. "Is there something wrong?"

"Keeping things from your mother isn't exactly right. It's deceitful. I never thought you were a deceitful boy." Connor held his breath not knowing what was coming

89

next. "I met Mrs Hubbard in the butcher's and she made me feel such a fool in front of the others in the shop. She told me how nice it was for you to be up at the Big House hobnobbing with Mr and Mrs Hughes. Having afternoon tea with them and looking at their books. She must have realised I knew nothing about it by the look on my face. She gave me a funny smile and said it was nice of them to take an interest. I was speechless! So are you going to tell me all about it then?"

Connor sighed but was relieved she hadn't found out about Morag. "I knew you'd find out eventually, but I didn't want to say anything straight away 'cos I knew you'd say I mustn't go. Mr Hughes saw me drawing down by the harbour and liked my drawings. He invited me up to the house to study his Art books. I've only been twice. This last time Mrs Hughes and I spent time in the garden drawing the plants, that's all. They think I could go far with my drawings and stuff."

"Oh it's them that have been filling your head with high-flying ideas. And are they going to pay for you to go to some fancy college? Because your father and I haven't got the money for you to go. You'd be better off giving up these daft ideas it'll only lead to disappointment. How can you have a future on the mainland with that leg of yours! You'll never manage on your own."

Her angry words crushed Connor. His happiness and hope faded, like smoke, his dreams in ribbons. He left the table, his meal unfinished, and stumped up the stairs.

Flinging himself on the bed, burying his face in the pillow, he let the tears of rage and misery flow out in an unstoppable flood. He hated himself, and his ridiculous leg, and for being a fool and allowing himself to dream and hope. His mother was right there was no escape for someone like him, he was just a cripple who would have to spend his life hobbling around the island with everyone feeling sorry for him. He thumped the pillow over and over again as the tears raced unchecked down his cheeks.

***

When his tears were spent and he lay exhausted and empty, the words Morag had spoken came back to him. Something about him being a great painter one day. She'd said it very casually, as if it was a foregone conclusion. Immediately he took heart and resolved not to give up his dreams just yet. They were worth fighting for. He turned onto his side and slept.

CHAPTER 20

When Connor arrived at breakfast the next day his father was sitting at the table too, looking very grim and tight-lipped. Connor braced himself for what was to come, and didn't sit down at the table. He could feel rage boiling up inside and fury towards this man who wanted to rob him of any self-respect and steal his future.

"Your mother's been telling me what you've been up to, hobnobbing with mainland people who should know better than filling a lad's head with daft ideas."

Connor's eyes blazed and he spat out the words at his father.

"They're not 'daft ideas'. They believe in me; they believe in my ability. They don't look at my leg like you do. They don't even see it. I'm a real person when I'm with them. Not a useless cripple, as you see me!" He heard his mother gasp and saw her hands fly to her mouth. His father's expression froze and Connor tried to read the look in his eyes, but gave up and turned for the door. Picking up his bag from the chair, he left.

He heaved a huge sigh, taking in the tangy, salty air. His head was ringing with all the things he wanted to say and all the things he wanted to hear his father say. He shook his head to try to untangle his jangling thoughts and by the time he had calmed down he found himself at the top of the steps down to the cove.

It was another lovely day, the sun beaming down and a gentle breeze sweeping across the short grass, bending the harebells. Now and again a small cloud would pass lazily overhead bringing with it a transitory shadow, dimming momentarily the bright colours of grass and flowers. Then out it came once more and Connor smiled to himself seeing it as a picture of his life at the moment… sunshine and shade… happiness and misery in equal measure.

He lay down and gazed up at the sky, his hands behind

92

his head, his eyes following the slow drift of the stiff-winged sea birds rising and falling effortlessly on the air currents. His ears catching their squawking and squabbling cries as they roosted on the narrow ledges of the cliffs.

He wasn't meeting up with Morag that afternoon, and then he remembered, he'd promised her a notebook and pen. He sat up and rummaged in his bag for his purse, where he put his tips; hoping it was there with the money still in it, and not transferred to the tin he kept on his windowsill.

He blew out a long breath of relief, it was still there, the coins jingling promisingly. He tipped the money out onto the back of his sketch pad and counted it carefully. He had five pounds fifty. If Connor had brought the rest of his money he would have been able to buy a new watercolour pad as well, but there was no way he was going to return home just yet.

Connor decided to walk to Gaelcreags and have a bite to eat there as well. He missed Danny. It would have been much more fun if Danny was with him. He sighed and set off after tipping the coins back in his purse and pushing it down into his bag.

The sun was very warm as he crossed the cliff top and began to walk with halting steps down the sloping path that led to Gaelcreags. The trek felt much longer on his own without the usual chatter that took place when Danny was with him, and he was hot and tired when he reached the outskirts of the town. Thankfully the buildings cast some shade.

He made his way to the store that sold everything; pots and pans, buckets and spades, biscuits and chocolates, felt-tips and pencils, pens and envelopes and notebooks. Connor soon found what he wanted and queued to pay. While he waited he heard his name called. Looking back, he saw Rory's cheerful face grinning at him. Connor grinned back.

93

"See you outside," Rory said.

Connor nodded, shoved his purchases into his bag and went outside to wait for Rory. He came out carrying a huge carrier bag.

"What have you got there?" Connor asked, curious.

"My sister's birthday. I've been saving my paper-round money. What's up with you and Danny? Haven't seen you around with him lately"

"Oh we had a 'fall out'. My fault!"

"What about? I can't imagine Danny getting too steamed up to fall out with you. You were always best mates."

"It was about the match. I missed the first bit of it and didn't see Danny's goal, Moira pointed it out to Danny and he just exploded at me. My mind was elsewhere that day."

"That's crazy! Moira's a nasty piece of work. She just wants Danny all to herself. I think he's getting fed up with her now, to tell the truth. He can't go anywhere without her! Are you stopping for something to eat?"

"I was thinking about it."

"What d'you fancy? Burger and chips?"

"Yeah, why not." Connor pulled out his purse and they wandered over to the burger bar then went and sat on the seawall munching away, Rory telling Connor all the gossip between mouthfuls.

"By the way," Rory said. "We're having a barbecue at Herring Quay beach on Saturday. We're using Susie's birthday as an excuse. Would you be able to come? Are you allowed to swim? It's a great bay to swim in. There's room in our car, we could pick you up."

Rory was always like this, rattling on from one thing to the next. He was hard to follow sometimes.

"Will Danny and Moira be there?"

Rory's face fell. "I have invited them. I expect you'll feel a bit awkward. Let me know by Friday night and we'll pick you up Saturday morning."

94

They spent the afternoon wandering in and out of the shops, Rory talking non-stop about his family, especially his little sister. His parents had divorced when he was quite young and his father had married again. Rory stayed with his Dad and got on well with his step-mum. Susie was his half-sister.

"Are you going to see your Mum this holiday?" Connor asked.

Rory puffed out his cheeks and wrinkled his nose. "I think I'll go for the last week of the holidays. It's actually not much fun. I always feel as if I'm interrupting their life and they don't know what to do with me. They haven't had any kids of their own. To be honest I think that was the problem between Mum and Dad. Dad wanted a family and Mum didn't. So she left."

"I didn't know that," Connor said.

"I don't talk about it much. It's not important anymore." He shrugged.

"It must have been awful at the time," Connor said.

"I was about three. I do remember crying a lot and longing for Mum, but Dad was always there for me and eventually I got over it. He's never talked badly about her or anything. I did ask him why not, a little while ago and he said he didn't want me to hate her, we're all different. Apparently she had a very unhappy childhood and he believes it affected her badly."

"That's amazingly generous of him," Connor exclaimed.

"The thing is, we're a happy family now and that's all that matters. My step-mum Jenny is lovely and Susie is incredible! You'll see on Saturday if you can come."

The afternoon was coming to an end and it was time to return home. Connor was dreading it. He had no idea what sort of a reception he would receive.

"You go on if you like Rory," he said as his limping pace was very slow.

Rory shook his head. "I'm in no hurry. What have you been up to anyway?" he asked.

Connor was not sure how much to share with Rory, they'd never been that close. Danny had been his one and only confidante, but Rory had shared with him for the first time some very personal stuff so he decided to tell him a bit about his row with his Dad and what he hoped to do with his life. For once Rory listened without interrupting.

"I did wonder whether things were OK with your Dad as he never turned up at any school evenings or came to the Art competition prize giving when you won first prize. I always thought he was out on the boat. Doesn't he like you painting?"

"No! he's disappointed that I'll not follow in his footsteps and become a fisherman like him."

"Well to be honest Connor, I'm really thrilled that you've made a stand and are determined to do something different, and you're good at it. But it can't be easy. I know I said I wasn't sure whether I wanted to be a fisherman like my Dad, and quite honestly, the way things are in the industry, I might have to think of something else too, but I hate studying. I wouldn't mind being a car mechanic. I've helped out at the garage with Old Gordon and he says I'm quite good at it."

"There you are then," Connor grinned at him. "We're all different and just because our Dads worked on the boats doesn't necessarily mean we have to."

Rory was grinning from ear to ear. "I'm not going to share this with anyone else though, are you?"

"I only ever shared stuff with Danny before."

"Oh Danny's OK. It's funny how you know who you can trust. I'd never tell Ewan anything." They both laughed as they walked down the hill into the village.

CHAPTER 21

Although Connor had been dreading facing his mother and father, neither of them mentioned the row that had happened that morning. His father was reading the paper and ignored Connor as usual, his mother was her ordinary self, fussing in the kitchen, then bringing their food to the table. Everything was back to normal as if nothing had happened.

The next morning Connor delivered two loads of ironing for his mother, then went straight to the cove. He wanted to swim on his own, worried that his courage would desert him if Morag wasn't there. But he had no need to worry. He stripped off his jeans and slid into the water which was high up the beach. He practised everything Morag had taught him and when he felt too cold he scrambled out and sunned himself on the steps before going back in once more. He couldn't dive though. His uneven legs caused him to topple sideways so he contented himself with leaning forwards, knees bent, arms stretched out in front and sliding into the water without making too much of a splash.

When it was lunchtime and his stomach was beginning to rumble, he climbed up to the cliff top, sat by his favourite rock and munched the sandwiches he had bought that morning from the cafe.

The tide was going out. silver rivulets ran down to the receding water carving channels in the wet sand which gleamed blue, reflecting the cloudless sky. A pair of puffins perched on a nearby rock which was surrounded with a wreath of delicate thrift in pink bloom. Connor pulled his sketch book from his bag and quickly sketched them filling in the background of cliffs, sky and sea when they flew off.

Having warmed up he made his way carefully down the steps once more. There was no sign of Morag but he went into the sea anyway and swam out to the rock, feeling thrilled that he had the courage to do it without her presence. He practised his own method of diving then noticed a seal swimming nearby and showing a lot of interest in his activities. He waved, knowing it was Morag. The seal swam towards the rock and then it was Morag, clambering up carrying her cloak.

"You're doing well. I like the new style of diving."

"I couldn't manage doing it the proper way. I kept falling over."

"Shall we swim further out? We can always rest on this rock on the way back."

They spent the rest of the afternoon swimming back and fore, resting for a while on the rock then off once more. Connor gaining strength all the time. Eventually they swam back to the beach and Connor wrapped himself in his towel, his teeth chattering. Morag spread her cloak over a large flat rock and they sat in the sunshine.

"It's freezing when you first go in and then you get used to it, and then it's really cold again. I'm glad it's so sunny, I warm up much quicker. By the way, I've got something for you," Connor said ferreting around in his bag. He pulled out the notebook and pen. "I got these for you yesterday."

Morag's eyes were round with delight. He showed her how the pen worked, as she had never seen one before, leave alone used one. He wrote her name on the first page then handed it to her.

"Go on, you have a go."

Morag took the pen, pressed the end so the point appeared and carefully copied her name beneath the letters Connor had written. Then looked up at him.

"What else shall I write?" She handed the pad back to him and he wrote out all the words that he had scratched in the sand. She took the pad back and began stringing words together to make simple sentences.

At this point, Connor looked up. A figure was making

his way down the steps towards them., it was Danny. Connor stood up not knowing what to expect.

"Hi Connor, I thought you might be here." He looked uncomfortable and wouldn't meet Connor's eyes. He had a piece of paper in his hand which he held out to Connor. It was a poster advertising a local Art exhibition to be held in the library at Gaelcreags the last week of the school holidays. "I thought you might be interested, you being a local artist," He paused, "look, I'm sorry about what I said. I was all het-up after the match. Can we be friends again?" He looked up hopefully.

Connor grinned. "I'm sorry too mate I shouldn't be so wrapped up in myself." He studied the poster then put it away in his bag. Connor clapped Danny on the shoulder and turning to Morag said "This is Morag by the way. She's been teaching me to swim."

"Hi," Danny said smiling. They budged up on the rock and Danny sat down beside them frowning in puzzlement as he caught sight of the notebook Morag was holding. "So," he continued looking at Connor's brown and well-toned body. "I thought you weren't allowed to swim. It's obviously doing you a lot of good. You look great!"

"My parents don't know."

Morag got up then. "I think I'd better go now," she said to Connor. "I'll put these in the cave. Thank you Connor. I'll practise when you're not here." She skipped over to the cave entrance and disappeared from view.

"Is she your girlfriend? Is she on holiday?"

"No and no! I'll tell you later," Connor mumbled as Morag emerged from the cave and walked towards them. She grabbed a corner of the cloak and tugged. The boys stood up, Danny looking curiously at the garment.

"Do you have a ball we could play with?" she asked Danny. His face creased in amusement.

"Yes," he said slowly.

"Could you bring it next time and we could play with

it?" He shook his head, biting his lip in puzzlement.

"Why not?"

"Wonderful! I'll look forward to it." she smiled and skipped off towards the sea looking back and waving before diving into the water.

"She's really weird!" Danny exclaimed looking at Connor and seeing his face tinged with embarrassment. "Where's she from?"

"Sule Skerry," Connor answered shortly. Danny cocked his head on one side.

"That's miles away. No-one lives there."

"You're not going to believe me," Connor said.

"Try me."

"She's a Selkie."

"A what!" Danny's eyes flew wide.

"I knew you wouldn't believe me."

"You'd better start at the beginning pal."

So Connor related everything that had happened including the lighting up of the cave, her ability to calm the sea, and what the cloak was all about.

Danny's breath escaped slowly, puffing out his cheeks. "It's a lot to take in... but I believe you. Why does she want to play with a ball?"

"She likes being on land and made friends with me hoping I'd play with her and then she saw my leg and so she showed me how to swim instead. I'm free in the water Danny. I feel I could do anything."

It was time to go. They chatted while Connor dressed.

"Are you going to Rory's Barbecue tomorrow. "Oh blast! I forgot to tell Morag. I'll write a note in her book." Connor limped over to the cave and found the notebook on the ledge and wrote 'sorry cannot come today' in big letters, then joined Danny again. "I'm teaching her to read and write," he said to Danny by way of explanation. "I met Rory yesterday and he invited me to the Barbecue. Will Moira be coming?"

100

Danny pulled a face. "I hope not. She's far too clingy. My life's not my own when she's around." They laughed together as they walked up the steps.

"Could you tell Rory I can come? He said he'd pick me up."

"Of course. No problem."

Connor's heart was as light as a feather, happy to be friends again.

Once in his room Connor took out the poster Danny had given him and studied it. Anyone could enter their work in the exhibition as long as they lived in the islands. There was no age limit but the paintings had to be entered a week before, to a selection panel who would choose the best ones to be exhibited. The paintings had to express aspects of life on the islands.

Connor was very thoughtful and a tiny flame of excitement sprang to life deep inside his being.

CHAPTER 22

Rory picked Connor up at two o'clock on Saturday afternoon. Mrs McKenzie's face was lined with anxiety as she followed him to the car, wiping her hands in her apron and peering in at the window giving him strict instructions to him to be careful. Rory's mother wound down the window and assured her that he would be well looked after.

"Rory's Dad will be in the water with them all the time and he's a great swimmer. There's no need to worry."

"But Connor doesn't swim," Connor's mother exclaimed.

"Don't worry, he'll be fine." And with a wave and a smile they were off, with Susie giggling in her car seat between the two boys. Connor sat back closing his eyes, red with embarrassment.

"You'll be OK when we go in the water," Rory said reassuringly. "You could just paddle or sit in the shallows."

"I can swim," Connor looked steadily at Rory. "She just doesn't know that." Rory's eyes opened wide. "I've been practising almost every day since we broke up. I knew that if I told her she'd flap and worry. So I didn't tell her."

"Where d'you go?" This was the tricky bit. Fortunately, Susie decided to join in the conversation at that moment, so Connor didn't have to answer him.

***

They all piled out of the car when they reached Herring Quay grabbing bags, sunshades, shrimping nets, folding chairs and all the accessories for an enjoyable time on the beach; not forgetting the hostess of the party --- Susie in her car seat.

102

Some of their friends, including Danny, had already arrived and had picked a good spot to pitch camp where the soft sand joined the firmer sand so sand castles could be built and parasols firmly planted to give shade.

The tide was just on the turn so as soon as everyone had arrived there was a general clamour to go into the sea.

"What would you like to do Connor while they're bathing?" Mrs Cameron, Rory's Mum, asked Connor.

"It's OK Mrs Cameron. I can swim. I just haven't told Mum." He smiled at her.

"Do you want a hand getting down to the sea?" Danny asked Connor softly, knowing he'd have difficulty once out of his special trainers.

"I'll keep my trainers on till I'm almost at the edge of the sea. If you could walk beside me and steady me if I wobble when I take them off, I should be fine. I've been practising walking too." Mr Cameron followed them down keeping a keen eye on Connor, glad that Danny was helping but not making a scene about it.

Danny and Connor reached the brink of the sea where there were gentle ripples and tiny lacy waves. Connor toed off his trainers with Danny's help and limped awkwardly into the deeper water, then launched himself into the waves and was off, cleaving the water with a powerful stroke that left the other boys staring in amazement. Danny was grinning and laughing delightedly. He chased after Connor who turned onto his back and floated, waiting for Danny to catch up.

"Wow! you told me you'd learnt to swim but not like a champion!" Danny said spitting out mouthfuls of salty water.

"She's a great teacher." Connor rolled onto his front and he and Danny swam together, parallel to the shore before turning back to join the others.

The other lads swam towards Connor with big grins on their faces, calling out comments.

"You're a dark horse Connor. Where did you learn to swim like that?"

"Look at you all brown and muscly. The girls will be falling over themselves when you get back to school."

"You'll have to enter the swimming competition next year."

Someone threw a beach ball into the midst of them at that point so they spent the next hour splashing about throwing and catching the ball. Connor was bursting with happiness, for the first time he felt part of the gang even though he knew it would only last till he got out of the water.

Mrs Cameron was calling to them that lunch was ready so they began to drift shore wards. Connor had one last swim out into deeper water. A lone seal was gliding, eyes and nose above the waves. It blew out a stream of bubbles as Connor swam closer, then swam towards him and nudged him with its nose, its mouth wide as if laughing. He reached and stroked its head.

"Hello Morag. I hope you got my message. Sorry I forgot to tell you." The seal nudged him again then turned and swam out to the open sea.

"Was that a seal?" a voice called out. Connor turned his head to see Mr Cameron a few yards away.

"Mr Cameron!" Connor gasped. "I didn't know you were still in the water."

"Said I'd keep an eye on you, but seeing how well you can swim, I'd say it was unnecessary. It was a seal wasn't it?"

"Yeah," agreed Connor. "A very tame one."

***

After their lunch of salad and sandwiches, Mrs Cameron produced a birthday cake with two candles, and they all

104

sang 'Happy Birthday' to a very excited Susie who clapped her hands and energetically blew the candles out, followed by shouts of joy. Everyone laughed at her enthusiasm.

The boys played team games and football in the afternoon but Connor sat in the sand with Rory and his little sister making sand castles, collecting shells and dried seaweed and decorating the castle walls. Susie was delighted. She wobbled about on her sturdy legs babbling away in a language that Connor didn't understand. She found Connor very interesting and when she was tired climbed into his lap demanding a story. Rory went to join the lads. Connor didn't mind reading to her and when she fell asleep Mrs Cameron lifted her gently and laid her down in her travel cot in the shade.

Connor took out his sketch book and began capturing the boys' antics as they played football. Mrs Cameron watched him greatly interested.

"I've never seen your drawings before. You're very skilful. How do you do it so quickly?" He gave her a brief smile.

"Practise."

Danny arrived and flopped down beside him reaching for a bottle of water that was in a bucket of cold sea water to keep it cool. He joined the conversation.

"He's going to enter some of his paintings in the Islands Exhibition at Gaelcreags this Summer. Aren't you Connor?" Danny looked at him pointedly and nudged him with his toe.

"As a matter of fact, I am," Connor replied flicking his sketch book shut, his blue eyes steady and determined.

"Have you seen his drawings, Mrs Cameron?"

"No, I'd like to. I used to do a bit of painting when I was younger and had the time." Danny took the sketch book from Connor and passed it over. She turned the pages, stopping at each one, smiling delightedly at the puffins and the lightning sketches of the boys, recognising

Rory instantly.

"You have a real talent there Connor. I'm sure you'll do well at the exhibition." She handed the book back.

Mr Cameron joined them and began organising a driftwood scavenge so they could make a fire and cook the sausages and foil-wrapped potatoes for their evening meal. Everyone got up to walk along the beach at the tideline searching for dry branches. Connor was left in charge of Susie watching, as she was still fast asleep.

He took out his pad once more and began to sketch the sleeping child.

CHAPTER 23

Mr Cameron placed large stones in a wide circle and piled the dry driftwood in the centre. The fire was soon roaring away and the sausages were held over the flames on long skewers. The potatoes placed in the ashes.

Connor noticed a change in the attitude the boys had towards him. He felt their respect for the first time. They didn't talk over him but listened when he had anything to say and they didn't treat him like an invalid.

They sat round the fire drinking bottles of coke and telling stupid jokes and stories about mischief they'd got away with at school, ending up singing songs they all knew from other camping experiences.

It was very late by the time they finished. The sun was going down into the sea spreading a gold and rose-red pathway across the waves, the colours rising and falling with the swell.

The cars to transport some of the boys home had arrived, so everything was packed up; the fire covered with sand to put it out, 'thank yous' and 'goodbyes' said. Rory's family and Connor were the last to leave the beach. It had been, for Connor, one of the best days of his life, and one, he knew, he would never forget.

***

His Father was still up when he arrived home. Connor's stomach clenched expecting a 'telling off'.

"Had a good time have you?" he asked gruffly.

"Yeah, very good thanks," Connor replied.

"You don't normally go out with all the lads."

"Yeah, well, Rory invited me. It was his sister's second birthday."

"A good man that Cameron, wants Rory to take over

his place on the boat, eventually, when he retires. Seems his new wife has other ideas though."

Same old story Connor thought. I'm not going to listen. He sighed.

"Mrs Cameron is very nice too. Anyway, I'm tired I'm going to bed." He made his way up the staircase feeling the weight of his Father's disapproval descend once more onto his shoulders.

***

Life settled into its normal pattern, delivering ironing and swimming with Morag, except that on Sunday afternoon Danny joined them. They swam, racing to the rock and back, then, as Danny had promised, they played with a football he had brought. Morag was very nimble, but hopeless at using her feet to kick the ball or dribble it. Connor sketched them, joining in their laughter. They returned to the sea and played catch with the ball. Connor joining in.

Back on the beach Connor asked Morag how she had found him on Saturday at Herring Quay.

"When you didn't come, I went to the cave and read your note. Herring Quay is the next bay. So I swam round and found you. It looked like great fun," she sighed wistfully.

"I didn't see you," said Danny, "You could have joined us."

Morag giggled. "I don't think so, but Connor recognised me."

"I gave her a pat on the nose," Connor said grinning.

Danny looked puzzled for a moment, then the light dawned.

"Oh! Oh I see. You weren't exactly... you were ... not yourself," he babbled going pink.

"I was my other self," Morag explained patiently and smiled at his embarrassment. "Can you come again tomorrow?" she asked. "That was so much fun."

"I can't come in the week. I help Dad in the shop now. He's offered to pay me. Next weekend though maybe?" Morag looked disappointed.

"You'll have to make do with me," Connor said, "but I could bring a ball and we could play in the sea if you like." Her face brightened.

"I'd like that. Till tomorrow then."

She picked up her cloak and trailing it behind her made her way to the sea. Danny and Connor dressed and climbed the steps home.

***

Tuesday afternoon was cloudy, but windy so Connor knew that soon the clouds would blow away and hopefully the sun would come out once more. His Mother frowned at him as he made himself ready to visit the Big House, gathering his paints and pencils and stowing them in his bag.

"I suppose you're off to the Big House," she stated shortly.

"Yep," Connor answered, slinging his bag over his shoulder and making for the door.

"You'll be sorry," she murmured shaking her head.

Connor didn't look back.

The wind whipped his face and tore at his curls which were now streaked with gold by the sun. In spite of the disapproval of his parents, things were changing for him. He was changing. He felt strong and deeply happy.

As soon as he met up with Mr and Mrs Hughes, he showed them the poster.

"My friend Danny gave it to me and thought I ought to

try and show some of my stuff. What do you think?" They both studied the poster.

"I think it's a great idea," Sasha said. "What do you think Thomas?"

"I have no idea of the standard of work but I don't see why you shouldn't attempt it. Of course the work has to be framed, but that's not a problem, we have a lot of spare frames hanging about somewhere. I'm sure we could find plenty for your work."

"Do you mean I really should enter more than one?" Connor asked in surprise.

"Of course, four or five at least maybe more. They might only choose two. But you have to show them a range of your work." Mrs Hughes stated smiling. "And it's not 'stuff' Connor it's your 'Work'." Connor blushed.

"Let's go through your sketch book and choose which ones to work on." Mrs Hughes was very business-like, all of a sudden, pushing the Art books to one side to make space for Connor's sketch book.

"I don't think you need me," said Mr Hughes. "I'll leave you to it. I must get on with my book."

Mrs Hughes turned the pages and reaching for a notebook that was on top of the bureau, began to make notes. When she saw the sketch of Susie she exclaimed "Oh Connor this is lovely. You must enter this. Have you ever used pastel?"

He shook his head.

Biting her lip, she said "We haven't got a lot of time, but I think you should have a go at doing this again only bigger, and in pastel. You can practise this afternoon to get used to them then take them home with you. I've got the right paper too."

She continued looking through his work and chose eight pictures that she felt stood a good chance of being included in the exhibition. Some, like the flower studies just needed framing as they were. Others, like the quayside,

110

the sketch of Dernvoe and the study of his mother doing the ironing needed enlarging and maybe transferred to another medium like acrylics. Again, Connor had no experience in acrylics.

"Well," she said, "I think we're going to have a fun afternoon! Come and join me in my studio."

Connor followed feeling bemused. Mrs Hughes was like a whirlwind... pastels, acrylics?

Her studio was the extension that they had had built. It faced north and there were huge skylights. The whole room, which was immense, was filled with a bright even light. Connor gazed, open-mouthed. There were easels, large drawing boards, a wide table and shelves stacked with pots containing all sorts of brushes and tubes of paint. The back wall was hung with examples of her designs, mannequins in glamorous clothes were placed around the room, and canvasses with fascinating patterns in brilliant colours of what Connor took to be fabric designs leant against the wall. He stood transfixed staring.

"Come on Connor. There's lots to do." She placed a pile of stiff paper in different colours on the wide table and brought from one of the shelves a large box containing what Connor thought was sticks of chalk. She chose a sheet of grey paper and began to draw using the chalks. She demonstrated all the various ways the sticks could be used as well as using her fingers to smudge the colours together.

"You don't have to cover every inch of paper," she said. "Let the paper show through and add to the texture. Do you see?"

Connor nodded thrilled by what he saw.

She shoved the paper towards him. "Come on your turn. You can use as many sheets as you like. Try all the colours if you want to." The afternoon sped by. He was totally absorbed and Mrs Hughes was delighted.

"You've got the right touch, and you've picked up the

111

technique really quickly. I suppose you have to go home now, and I wanted to show you how to use acrylics. Connor, would you be able to come over in the evenings? There's plenty of light up to ten o'clock at the moment."

Connor beamed "That would be amazing. I'd love to, if you can spare the time."

"Good, that's settled then. I'll tell Thomas. He'll be thrilled." She loaded Connor up with the coloured sheets of pastel paper and the box of pastels.

"I can't manage Wednesday night," she said. "but Thursday and Friday will be fine, and I'll introduce you to acrylics." She was smiling broadly. "You've no idea how much pleasure this gives us." She said as they walked to the front door.

"I'm really grateful," Connor replied, his blue eyes blazing with gratitude. "You are the first people to show any interest at all, and I'm learning so much already."

"Till Thursday then."

CHAPTER 24

Connor worked hard all Wednesday evening reproducing his drawing of Susie. Carefully choosing the right shade and texture of paper. At first he was too heavy-handed with the pastels and he had to try several times before he completed the drawing to his satisfaction. The paper showed through in places and he had rubbed and smudged the colour in her curls so they blended in, adding to the dreamy quality of her round sleeping face. Mrs Hughes had given him a fixative spray to use when he was completely happy with what he had produced. It was gone midnight when he finished.

For the first time Connor felt his life had meaning and purpose. Every afternoon he met with Morag and they swam together. Sometimes she leant him her cloak and he became a seal swimming far out into the ocean and plunging into the depths skimming the rocky floor of the sea and once he caught an eel. He felt it wriggle in his mouth, but he couldn't swallow it and spat it out. Morag laughed and laughed when he told her. It was not something he wanted to repeat.

Thursday evening, Mr Hughes had already found frames for Connor's flower studies. They looked so professional surrounded by a suitable mount and frame. Connor could hardly believe they were his paintings. When he showed the pastel drawing of Susie, Mrs Hughes was very impressed. She called her husband.

"Look Thomas, Connor's first attempt at pastel. It's going to need a very special frame."

"Mmm, something quite deep I think, but not too dark a mount. I think I've got the very one. Leave it with me. Well done Connor, it's a fine piece of work."

Connor spent the rest of the evening messing about with the acrylic paints. He realised he could use them like watercolours, but it was much more fun to use them thick

113

as if they were oil paints. The only thing was, they were very quick to dry so he had to be pretty sure about what he was doing.

After a while Mrs Hughes gave him a fairly large blank canvas and a palette knife.

"Would you like to have a go at one of your seascapes using the palette knife? I think you could capture those threatening clouds very well."

So Connor tried, swirling the paint, stippling it to capture the spray of the waves, completely lost in the colour and texture, oblivious to his surroundings. Mrs Hughes watched in amazement, a lump in her throat and tears threatening. The boy was a true artist, completely lost in the moment, giving himself totally to the work before him.

At last Connor stood back to study what he had done. It was as if he was rousing from a dream. He gave a long sigh blowing out his breath, and wiped a hand across his forehead, then realised Mrs Hughes had been watching him. He gave a tentative smile and raised his eyebrows, asking silently for her opinion.

She walked slowly towards him. "Connor, that is remarkable!"

Connor blushed. He felt very tired as if he'd swam to the rock and back three times over.

Mrs Hughes's face was filled with wonder, as her eyes raked the painting from top to bottom.

"I don't know how you've done it, on your first attempt, but the whole picture is complete and so full of energy and life. I can almost smell the ozone and feel the wind whipping up those waves. I love it!"

"I've never done anything like this before. It's great to feel so free with the paints. It looks a bit abstract to me though. Maybe people won't 'get' what it's about."

"Just because it's not photographically precise doesn't mean people won't appreciate it or understand what

114

you've done. There will always be people who won't like your work. You've just got to carry on and do what you believe in."

"My word Connor! That's a beauty!" Mr Hughes had come into the studio. "Another one for the exhibition?"

"D'you really think so? I felt as if I was just experimenting. I think I ought to put more work into it."

"Well maybe on the next one. I thought I'd show you this before you go home." Mr Hughes turned the picture he was holding towards Connor. He had framed the pastel of Susie. The gilt frame and soft grey mount made the sleepy face of Susie glow with life.

Connor gasped. "That's lovely! Thank you so much Mr Hughes it's transformed the picture somehow."

"No, just brought out what was already there... Did you know it was ten o'clock young man?"

"Oh," Connor said. "I'd better be off. Can I hang onto the pastels, there's another one I'd like to do?"

"Of course. I can't manage tomorrow Connor, how about Saturday?" Mrs Hughes asked smiling.

"That'll be fine." Connor walked home in the glimmering twilight breathing in the evening air that was scented with the salty spray of the sea. He felt complete and totally fulfilled.

In his room, he took out his sketch book and turned to the drawing of his mother. He wanted to produce another pastel picture that would complement the one of Susie. They would be a pair... a baby and an older Mother. He worked till Midnight but couldn't produce the effect he was after so, set it aside to continue the next evening.

CHAPTER 25

The days whizzed by, afternoons spent swimming with Morag and most evenings at the Big House painting. The day for the submitting of the paintings was looming. Mr and Mrs Hughes helped Connor choose which ones to enter. They chose six in the end.

"Isn't that too many?" Connor asked pulling a nervous face.

"No, no no," Mr Hughes assured him. "They might not take them all. We'll see."

On the Friday the paintings were loaded carefully into the back of the car and they all drove over to the library at Gaelcreags. Connor stayed in the car, while Mr and Mrs Hughes carried the paintings inside. He was too nervous, thinking how awful he'd feel if they said he was too young. They were back out in no time at all.

"They're going to assess all the work and email me to collect any that are not needed. It's a good job we made you sign all your paintings Connor, they thought they were mine and were going to write my name down in the catalogue." Mr and Mrs Hughes laughed aloud. "I could understand them thinking the work was yours Sasha, But me!" He continued to chuckle.

For the next few days Connor kept wondering how many of his paintings would be rejected. Both Danny and Morag did their best to cheer him up and Connor made a valiant effort to put the exhibition out of his mind, but it hung there in the back of his mind like a threatening black cloud.

When Tuesday afternoon came he dragged himself up to the Big House expecting the worst.

"Why the long face?" Mrs Hughes teased smiling.

"Have you heard from the library?" Connor was almost trembling with anxiety.

"We have Connor." And before she could continue he

interrupted.

"Which ones didn't they want?"

Mrs Hughes laughed, shaking her head in disbelief. "You have got to start believing in yourself. They accepted them all, of course!"

Connor's mouth dropped open. He was stunned. "All of them? All six?"

"Yes, they really liked them and were glad to have a new local painter to add to the usual crowd. This calls for a celebration, don't you think?" Mr Hughes joined them and they opened a bottle of wine for themselves and sparkling elder flower for Connor.

The exhibition was to be open to the public the following Saturday, but they could go to the private view on the Friday night. All the other artists would be there. Connor was unsure about attending a grown up affair and really didn't want to go.

"Of course you don't have to go if you don't want to Connor," said Mrs Hughes sympathetically. "It will be full of stuffy adults. We've been given two invites so Thomas and I can go together if you'd prefer. We can listen in to what people say about your work and tell you later."

"I don't think I want to know," Connor replied with a wry face.

***

Now that the exhibition was sorted out successfully Connor put it out of his mind. On the way home from the Big House he called into the shop to tell Danny the good news. Danny was thrilled and the whole family intended going over to Gaelcreags the following Sunday to view Connor's work.

Morag was pleased too when Connor told her on the Wednesday afternoon, but she seemed a bit subdued and preoccupied.

117

"What's up?" Connor asked her.

"Well," she hesitated, "I'd like to see your paintings too but I daren't go that far inland."

"You've seen most of them. They're from my sketch book… just bigger and in colour. That's not the whole problem though is it?"

She shook her head and sighed. "My little sister Shelly's gone missing."

"Missing? How d'you mean?"

"The whole family were out catching eels, spread over a wide area as usual and when we all arrived home, she wasn't with us anymore. We waited and waited for her to arrive but she didn't. All night, we waited hoping she'd return in the morning, but she didn't come. I'm really worried Connor, she's not very old. We all went back to look for her this morning, but there was no trace."

"Do you want to go out now and look for her? I'll come with you." Morag shook her head.

"It's too far for you to swim. You'd have to wear the seal cloak and I haven't another one… Connor, I'm sorry I can't stay today I must go back and look again. I'll see you tomorrow." Connor grabbed her arm and gave it a little shake.

"You'll find her, I know you will, try not to worry." Morag smiled a small tight smile and walked into the waves wrapping the cloak around her. A young seal ploughed through the waves towards the distant horizon.

Connor racked his brains as to what might have happened to Morag's little sister. He hadn't heard any news of a seal cull, and as far as he knew there were very few seal predators in the area. Maybe she was just lost, swam too far away from her family and when they all turned for home she was left behind.

A storm was moving in from the east and the sky had turned a charcoal grey, smudged with deep purple and black threatening clouds. The sea heaved leaden shoulders

118

streaked with scribbles of creamy white where the waves broke. Connor made his way up the steps heading for home.

CHAPTER 26

There was no news of Morag's sister Shelly on the Thursday afternoon.

"The thing is Connor, I'm sure I saw Shelly's cloak tucked behind a rock in my uncle's cave. It has a distinctive white shape like a shell on the shoulder."

"Did you ask him about it?"

"No," she gave a little shiver, "I don't like him very much. He's always been a bit of a bully and he resents the fact that my father is the leader, disagreeing with my father's peaceful attitude towards the fishermen of the village. The thing is, Connor, if it is her cloak then she is trapped somewhere as a human. I can't bear the thought of it!"

"Why would he do that?"

"I don't know," she shrugged.

"You ought to tell your father."

"I would if I was really sure, but I'd need to get hold of the cloak to prove it. That's what I ought to do first."

"Morag, if he's as nasty as you say, you'll have to be very careful. You don't want him catching you as well."

"I'll find a way to sneak into his cave when he's out catching eels. Don't worry, I will be careful," she assured Connor as she saw the worried expression on his face.

They swam for some of the time but both of them were thinking about Morag's dilemma and soon went back to the beach. All the bubble and sparkle that was Morag had disappeared.

"I'll teach you to write some messages," Connor suggested, as soon as he was dressed and dry. Morag went and retrieved her notebook from the cave.

"First I'll write a list of words that you might want to put in a message." He wrote, in her note book: sister, uncle, cloak, father, safe, help, found, danger, tomorrow, today, tonight. And then a few messages; 'Sister safe,' 'sister found,' 'meet Morag on beach tomorrow,' 'told father all well.'

"I don't think I've covered everything but if you can put your message in the cave. I could come every day and check. I'll be going back to school soon and won't be able to come in the afternoons any more, but we could meet in the evenings, it'll still be quite light, if you like."

"I would like it if we could still meet up, once I've found my sister, and I will leave messages for you."

Morag copied the words and phrases several times until she knew them by heart then returned them to the cave.

"I must go back now. Thank you Connor it's lovely to have a good friend I can trust." To Connor's surprise she flung her arms around him and gave him a hug. He grinned at her.

"That's what friends are like. Take care and let me know what happens." She picked up her cloak and walked towards the sea.

Connor decided to go up to the Big House and ask if it was alright for him to do some more painting. He felt restless and on edge. Morag's news was upsetting and made him feel helpless once more, a feeling he hadn't had for quite some time.

Connor was working on a painting of Morag dancing on the beach, celebrating the joy of movement. The work was delicate, but vibrant with life, emanating joy. It made Mrs Hughes smile every time she looked at it.

Mr Hughes brought up the subject of the 'Private Viewing' that was to happen on Friday night. Connor was adamant he wouldn't attend. In fact, he admitted he hadn't told his parents anything about it. Mr and Mrs Hughes were concerned, but Connor assured them his parents were not interested and it would only make his father angry if he knew.

"You will have to tell them soon Connor," Mr Hughes insisted.

"Maybe after the exhibition," Connor conceded reluctantly.

***

He decided to visit the exhibition on his own on Saturday morning. He didn't want any of the officials to know that he was one of the artists. He was afraid they would be angry if they knew he was a school boy and somehow disqualify him from the exhibition. Although no age limit had been mentioned in the poster.

It was almost lunchtime by the time he arrived and the library was quite full. The pictures were hung in a special room that was long like a gallery. Display boards were set up down the middle on which smaller paintings were displayed and it was here Connor found his watercolour studies. For some reason red dots had been stuck to the frames which puzzled him. What did they mean? Had they found out he was only fourteen and were warning people? But then he noticed some other artists had red dots on their frames too.

He moved on around the room stopping to look at the other paintings. There were plenty of seascapes, which wasn't a surprise as this was an island. Some very stiff portraits of presumably, notable people of the town, and some beautiful studies of plants and wild life.

Two paintings in particular seemed to be creating a lot of interest. Connor pushed his way through the crowd to see what they were looking at. He froze as he realised they were his seascapes, done with the palette knife in acrylics. They stood out amongst all the other paintings, he had to admit that. They were so lively they almost spoke! The people were whispering their comments to each other and pointing. Some were smiling in delight others frowning in concentration.

He walked on, his heart thumping in his chest, part of him felt proud at seeing his signature C.M. in the corner, but there was still a bit of him that felt anxious. What was he getting himself into?

In the far corner he came upon his two pastel drawings, Susie and his Mum ironing. He stared at them again. It had taken him a long time to capture his mother just the way he wanted, but he had done it in the end. Her face looked careworn, with tiredness around her eyes but her mouth set in determined lines as she swished the iron across the fabric. It was a tender portrait full of understanding and love. Again each picture had a red dot on the frame. He had to find out what they meant.

There was a man standing near the entrance to the gallery selling catalogues.

"Excuse me," Connor asked. "What do the red dots mean on some of the paintings?"

"That means they're sold lad. Did you want to buy one?"

"No, no thank you. I just wanted to know." He gave a brief smile. It had not entered his mind that anyone would want to pay for his paintings. Mr Hughes had not discussed it with him, but it must have been him who had put a price on them. Four paintings... maybe he would get twenty pounds! Five pounds each! Wow! He'd give it all to his Dad to show him that drawing was not a worthless occupation. Maybe he would change his mind about Connor going to college. His mind fizzed with excitement.

He crossed the road and bought himself a huge sandwich and sat on the seafront munching contentedly and dreaming about a rosy future with Mum and Dad proud of him.

CHAPTER 27

Morag returned to her uncle's cave to make sure that the cloak she saw was definitely her sister's. She'd just pulled it out from behind the rock and spread it wide when she heard a noise behind her. It was her uncle.

"So glad you came back. I thought you might." He looked so pleased with himself. "I'll have that young lady." He tore the cloak out of her hands, smirking at her, his eyes glistening with malice.

"Where is she? What have you done with my sister?"

"she's quite safe... for now. But that of course depends on you."

"What do you mean?"

"Oh my dear, have you any idea what a powerful weapon you possess? And you use it to play with your little friends... oh yes I know all about your Human friends. Whatever would your father do if he knew about them?"

Morag's face froze in alarm. "You know what would happen."

"Yes banishment! Never to see your dear family again. If you help me of course they need never know about your human friends and your dear little Shelly will be returned safe and sound."

"What do I have to do? What power have I got?"

"You can make waves, very big waves if you wanted to. In fact, enormous tidal waves that would sweep over the island and the town and wash away all the people who destroyed my only chance of happiness." He was waving his arms around in great theatrical gestures, a mad glitter in his eyes.

Morag gasped terrified. "I couldn't do that!" She appealed to him. "Uncle it wasn't the island people who killed Aunt Fiona. She became tangled in a net. It wasn't a deliberate act."

"You don't understand; all humans are killers at heart."

124

His face grew hard. "If you won't help me then I'm afraid your little sister will die. You'll never find her." He turned his back on Morag as if to leave the cave.

"No, no tell me what you want me to do." There was a short silence as they stared at each other.

"When the Spring tides are rising I want you to create a tidal wave to wipe out every human on the island and destroy every town and village as if they had never been. Only then will I return your sister's cloak and tell you where you can find her. And you will need this cloak to rescue her," he said raising it on high, "and until then, it will be hidden in the last place you would think to look. Now go from here till I summon you. Make sure you tell no-one or you know what will happen. I will send a messenger."

***

Sunday afternoon Danny joined Connor at the cove.

"You've sold some of your pictures then," Danny's smile stretched wide across his face, his eyes twinkling. "How much do you think you'll get for them?"

Connor's breath puffed out slowly. He shrugged. "I've no idea. I didn't put a price on them, Mr Hughes did. I didn't even realise people would be there to buy them."

Danny burst out laughing and slapped him playfully across the top of his head. "You really are an idiot sometimes. That's what exhibitions are all about. Didn't you know that?"

Connor shook his head. "I just like painting, didn't think about what the exhibition was for really." He looked out to sea. "I wonder where Morag is. I'll go to the cave and see if she's left me a message." Danny followed.

"I haven't seen this cave yet."

"It'll be too dark to see much, but the rock shelf where

125

she keeps her notebook is near the front so there might be enough light there."

They entered the cave and Connor felt along the shelf till he found the notebook. Danny had wandered further in.

"I had no idea this was here. D'you think Morag will light it up for us when she comes?"

"We can ask her." They stumbled out into the sunshine and Connor flipped open the book, but there was no message.

"Shall we go for a swim anyway?" Danny asked.

"Yep, maybe she's just late."

They left their clothes high up out of the reach of the tide and entered the icy waves heading for the rock, racing each other. Danny got there first this time.

"Come on slow-coach! What's up with you today?"

Connor pulled himself up beside Danny and shared with him everything Morag had told him. Just then, a seal nudged their dangling legs causing them to yelp in surprise. The seal materialised into Morag as she removed her cloak. Connor leant over and pulled her up. She looked very distressed. Her hair was wild and hanging in untidy tangles around her neck. Her eyes red as if she had been crying.

"I was just beginning to worry about you," said Connor. "What's up? You look awful! I've told Danny a bit of what you told me. I hope you don't mind. What's been going on?"

"I don't mind, I'm going to need all the friends I can get, although I don't know how you can help. Can we go back to the beach? I'll tell you everything in the cave." Her voice was shaking with anxiety.

They slipped into the water from the rock and swam back to the shore. Grabbing their clothes, they followed Morag into the cave. She muttered her little mantra again and the walls glowed once more. Danny was astonished, walking about and touching the walls gently with his

126

fingers as if he hoped the colour would rub off onto them.

When they were seated on a flat rock in the middle of the cave, Morag told them all she had discovered.

The boys were appalled.

"Can you do that? Can you really make waves?" Danny asked, his eyes round with horror.

"She's made waves for me to practise swimming in," Connor answered.

"What are we going to do? We'll have to warn the villagers and evacuate the island!"

"Hang on," Connor put out a restraining hand and grabbed Danny's arm. "It's not going to happen yet. We've got some time. Let's think about this. We must try to find Morag's sister. If we can rescue her, then your uncle won't have any power over you." He turned towards Morag. She was wiping her eyes on the hem of her cloak. "Cheer up we've got to work out a plan. Have you asked any other sea creatures if they've seen anything of your sister?"

Morag swallowed the last of her tears and sat up straighter. "I can ask the seals, the porpoises and dolphins." She said, her face beginning to brighten.

"And what about birds, can you talk to birds?" Danny broke in with enthusiasm. "They can fly for miles."

"Oh yes," she clapped her hands with delight. "The ospreys and the gannets are all my friends as well as the gulls. Oh Danny what a great idea!" She was beaming now.

"I don't think you should tell them the whole story," Connor warned, "in case your uncle talks to them and finds out. Tell them to report any findings only to you. You might have to make something up." Morag nodded gravely.

"I'll meet you here tomorrow afternoon as usual."

"Don't forget to let me know what's going on," Danny said to Connor.

"We can meet Monday evening if you like." They left the cave, Morag towards the sea and the boys towards the steps.

CHAPTER 28

Morag and Connor met up on Monday afternoon. They went straight to the cave.

"My uncle's been following me," Morag explained. "I don't want him to see us together. Although I don't suppose it matters now." She was very dispirited.

"Did you manage to get the word out to all the sea creatures and birds?"

"As many as I could, and I asked them to spread the word to other creatures and birds. So now, it's just a matter of waiting for news."

"I've been thinking," Connor said. "You'll have to have Shelly's cloak so she can transform into a seal and swim away."

"Exactly, but I haven't found it yet."

"Keep looking, and when you find it you'll be able to rescue her. Once you know where she is."

"I have to go Connor, maybe there'll be some news."

Connor swam about on his own for a while but missed Morag's company so left the sea, dressed and went home.

That evening he met up with Danny only to tell him Shelly hadn't been found.

***

Connor spent the morning catching up on his homework as he was starting back at school the following Monday. He found it hard to concentrate as his mind kept roving back to Morag and her sister Shelly. He wouldn't be seeing her today as it was Tuesday and he was due up at the Big House in the afternoon.

Mrs Hughes was introducing him to various techniques with brushes and palette knife and showing him how to use the acrylic paints like watercolour. He was doing some flower studies using acrylics and loving the vibrant colours.

129

"We have to go to the gallery tomorrow evening Connor to pick up any unsold work and collect any payment," Mr Hughes informed Connor.

"I didn't think anyone would want to buy them, but some have sold. I'm surprised."

"And pleased too, I hope." Mr Hughes raised his eyebrows.

Connor's face was lit up with a dazzling smile.

***

That night though, all his happy thoughts and feelings disappeared as he had another blazing row with his father.

"You've really disgraced this family now boy," his father said to him as soon as he walked through the door.

"What d'you mean?" Connor asked, immediately on the defensive.

"That Colonel Bannister's been over to Gealcreags and saw your scribblings in some exhibition in the library. How could you do such a thing parading your fanciful ideas in public? What are people going to think?"

Connor sighed and closed his eyes momentarily to calm the rage that was flaring up inside him.

Opening his eyes, he said, "D'you know what? I really don't care what you or anyone else thinks. I'm never going to stop painting. It's my life, and I know you'll never understand it. So you'd just better get used to it."

He was shaking by the time he reached his room. The awful thing was, he did care, he really wanted his parents to be proud of him and share his joy. But that was not going to happen any time soon, if ever.

***

130

The next morning at breakfast, Connor ate his cereal in silence watching his mother smooth away the creases in the tablecloths so expertly, wishing the creases of his thoughts and feelings could be smoothed out as easily.

"You mustn't be too hard on your Dad." His mother spoke softly. "He's very worried at the moment. The fishing's no good and the men are talking about selling the boat and getting shore jobs. The trouble is, your Dad is a lot older than the rest of them and he hasn't any other skills, so it's hardly likely he'll get a shore job. And the money I make isn't anywhere near enough to keep us going. So try and understand Connor, it's hard for him when the way of life he's always known, that went on for generations, is coming to an end."

"I had no idea," Connor whispered. "He must be really broken up. And I haven't helped have I?"

"You weren't to know. Your Dad wanted it kept from you."

"I'm sorry Mum, I really am."

Mrs McKenzie folded the last tablecloth and put it carefully into a bag. "These are for the B and B in Foyle Street, and these for the pub." She reached down another bag from the dresser and handed him two bags to deliver.

***

The delivery done, he wandered down to the quayside and sat watching the hustle and bustle of the tourist boat as it unloaded its passengers. They would comb the narrow streets looking for souvenirs, have lunch in the pub or the hotel and eventually make their way back to catch the next boat to the main island or the boat that would take them on to the next island.

Carrickquays' tourist trade had increased this Summer because of the quaintness of the harbour and the dramatic

131

cliffs that shadowed Dernvoe cove.

He met Danny briefly that evening as there was no sign of Morag again and so no news, then went on to meet Mr and Mrs Hughes.

The library was in a flurry of activity as the exhibitors were taking down their unsold paintings and envelopes of cheques and cash were being handed out. Everybody looked pleased with themselves as it had been a very successful exhibition, with people from the mainland, and the press being very interested. Photographs had appeared in the paper which had encouraged even more people to visit.

Connor and Mr Hughes made their way to the main desk as they were unable to find any of Connor's work. Mr Hughes asked politely if the paintings had already been taken down and put somewhere awaiting collection.

"Oh Mr Hughes, they have indeed, been collected already." The attendant beamed.

"By whom?" Mr Hughes frowned in consternation.

"Why, by the buyers of course. They were here at six o'clock precisely." The attendant looked at his watch. "It is eight o'clock now. Your artist friend was the most successful exhibitor, and all his work was sold. I have the money here for you," he said handing Mr Hughes a white envelope. "If you'll just sign the register."

"Maybe my 'artist friend' should do the honours," Mr Hughes smiled, handing the pen to a bewildered Connor. The attendant's mouth flew open and his eyebrows almost disappeared into his hairline.

"Are, are you the artist?" he stammered.

"Yes, I'm Connor McKenzie." He signed his name, gave a brilliant smile and limped proudly, head erect, out of the gallery with Mr Hughes, clutching the envelope.

CHAPTER 29

Back at home that evening Connor spread the money out on his bed and stared at it. One hundred and sixty pounds! Forty pounds each for the two acrylics! A cheque written out in his name, bought by the same man! He couldn't believe it. Mr Hughes had priced the paintings and had said they were all actually under-priced as it was only a small local exhibition. If it had been held on the mainland in a larger gallery, he would have put a higher price on them.

"Your work is good, Connor," he had said. "Believe me, I have artist friends and know excellent work when I see it."

***

So now, what to do with the money. At home in his room, all sorts of ideas spun round his head, but one thing was certain, he would offer it to his father, to prove to him that painting was a profitable occupation.

He gathered up the notes and went back downstairs. His father was reading the paper, listening to the radio. Connor cleared his throat loudly, suddenly feeling rather nervous.

"Dad, I've got something to show you." His father looked up briefly.

"Oh yes. What's that then?"

Connor spread the money on the table and waited. Eventually his father raised his eyes and was transfixed.

"Where did you get that?" His voice tight with suspicion.

"The exhibition. I sold all my paintings." The paper rustled down onto his father's lap.

"Your paintings?"

"Yes, my scribbles. It seems some people really like

them and are willing to pay good money for them. I want you to have this." Connor brushed the money across the table in his father's direction.

"I don't need your money. Those people have more money than sense it seems to me." He picked his paper up once more.

Frustration welled up in Connor and bitter disappointment.

"I just want you to know that I can make a good living out of my work.

"Pah!" His Dad cried. "That's not work!"

Connor's shoulders drooped. He stared at the money feeling hopeless. How was he to get through to this stubborn man? He made his way back upstairs leaving the money on the table.

He must have fallen asleep because he was woken by loud voices, arguing. His Mum and Dad were having a row! They never rowed. His Mum was, on the whole, too timid. She didn't sound timid now. He couldn't quite make out what was being said, the walls and floors of the cottage being too thick, but there was no doubt about the tone. He could pick out his mother's high angry voice, and his Father's indignant retorts that surprisingly changed into subdued gravelly tones, under his mother's tirade. When things quietened down Connor went back to sleep.

In the morning his mother handed him the money.

"Well done Connor," she said. "I'm proud of you. You'll have to open a bank account to pay in that cheque. You'd best go over to Gaelcreags this morning and get it done." To Connor's horror his eyes filled with tears and he slumped down at the kitchen table and sobbed, burying his head in his arms. His mother went to him reaching down and rubbing his back to soothe him. He gasped and hiccoughed trying to gain control.

"It's all I ever wanted," he choked out, "for you to be proud of me... I thought Dad would be proud of me." He raised wet, red eyes to his mother's face.

"He's a stubborn old fool and I've told him so. He'll come round now. You'll see. Now eat your breakfast and get off to Gaelcreags."

***

Thinking on his mother's words, it was with a much lighter heart that Connor made his way into Gaelcreags that morning. He arrived at the bank and paid in most of the money keeping some back to buy a new watercolour pad. He treated himself to his favourite sandwich and sat gazing out across the tiny harbour that was already busy with disembarking tourists. There were dolphins in the bay leaping and playing among the choppy waves and his thoughts turned to Morag, wondering how things were with her family problems and whether she'd found out where her sister was.

He remembered it would be his mother's birthday soon, and the pastel he had done for her had been sold, so he would have to do another one. Maybe he'd try acrylics, but use them like watercolours. His head was buzzing with ideas. When he reached the hill that led up to the cliff top he stopped, sat down, and began to sketch Gaelcreags.

Connor went straight to the cave and found Morag's notebook. There was a message of sorts: 'No come afternoon come evening meet.' From this Connor understood that they were to meet in the evening, not the afternoon. He replaced the notebook and went in search of Danny to see if he could come as well. He finished work at about six o'clock.

The shop was crowded with tourists, but Danny managed to slip out to talk to Connor for five minutes.

"It's like a mad-house in there!" Danny exclaimed. "We've never had so many tourists. They love the boat

135

trips from the mainland and do a tour of the islands." He drew breath. "What's up? Any news?"

"A message from Morag to meet her tonight. She couldn't come this afternoon. I thought we could go together."

"Great. I can make it. What time?"

"Half six… seven?"

"Make it seven, then I can have some dinner."

"OK. See you then." They parted and Connor made his way to the Big House hoping it would be alright for him to start the painting for his mother's birthday.

The Hughes were surprised to see him but welcomed him in none the less especially when he explained why he had come. Mrs Hughes was working on some new designs for fabrics.

"Just get what you need Connor. You know where everything is." So he set to work using his original pencil sketch as a guide.

At four o'clock Mr Hughes wandered in with a tray of tea and cakes.

"Time for a break. How are things Connor? Parents pleased?"

"My Mum is," Connor hesitated, remembering the painful episode of the morning.

"Your Dad still a problem?" Mr Hughes sighed. "Would it help if I had a word?"

"I don't think so." Connor shook his head. "Mum said this morning that he would come round eventually." He sighed.

***

At seven o'clock that evening the boys met on the beach. Connor was skimming flat stones into the water and counting how many times they bounced before sinking,

136

when Danny joined him. They had a competition. Danny finally won with five skips before sinking. They went to sit outside the cave to wait for Morag. They had no idea what time she would arrive.

"How much money did you make then?" Danny asked, coming straight to the point.

Connor took a deep breath. "A hundred and sixty pounds."

"You're kidding me!"

"No, I told you Mr Hughes priced them all. I'd never have put those prices on them."

"You're something else! D'you know that? You're friends with a Selkie and make a fortune out of a few paintings." Danny burst out laughing slapping Connor on the back in delight. "What are you going to do with it?"

"I've put it in the bank for now."

"I bet your Mum and Dad are thrilled."

"Huh! Fat chance!" said Connor, and went on to tell Danny about his conversation with his Dad and the row he'd overheard later.

"I'm sorry pal. My parents would be thrilled, telling everyone how marvellous I was."

"Yeay, you're lucky. Here comes Morag." She was running up the beach dragging her cloak behind her. She flopped down beside them to catch her breath.

"We'd better go in the cave. I don't want my uncle's spies to see me." They followed her, and once the cave was lit up, made their way to the big flat rock in the middle and sat down.

"What's been happening?" Danny asked.

"I'm pretty sure she's on Sula Sgeir. One of the gannets told me an old grey seal swims into a cave regularly every night with a strange box-like container then collects it in the morning. It must be food for my sister. Shelly must be confined inside that cave so she can't be seen. The thing is, my uncle is keeping a very close eye on me now, and that's why I haven't been able to meet you. I think he will be making use of me very soon. I can't rescue her yet because I haven't found her cloak."

"Is there anything we can do?" Connor was frowning.

"If my uncle decides I'm a danger to his plans, he might take my cloak away from me and I won't be able to rescue Shelly, but if I managed to bring you a Selkie Cloak Connor, and, when I find it, Shelly's cloak, then you could rescue her for me."

"But that's just a back-up plan right?" Connor was looking distinctly nervous.

Morag frowned "Back-up?"

"Yeah if the first plan doesn't work we use the next plan."

Morag smiled. "Oh I see, yes. If I can't rescue her, you will. I'll try to get another cloak to you. When Selkies grow old and die sometimes, their cloaks are left behind. The thing is, if I am trapped by my uncle and you manage to rescue Shelly, how will I know I can stop making the wave?"

"I know what we can do," Danny cut in excitedly. "We can light the beacon." They looked at him blankly. "You know, at the top of the cliff. We can build a huge bonfire. It'll be seen from the sea for miles. We can light it as soon as we know Shelly is safe!"

"That's brilliant Danny!" Connor exclaimed. "You can do that once I've rescued Shelly. We must get hold of her Selkie cloak though."

"Well that's what I'm trying to do. I've looked everywhere." Morag's small round face was crumpled in concern.

"Look, I can come down to this beach every day," said Connor, "to check if any cloaks have been delivered. I'll need both if I'm to do the rescue. How will I know which is which, apart from size maybe?"

"Shelly's has a white shell shape on the side. It's

138

unmistakable." The plan was assembled, they just needed the two cloaks to be ready to carry it out.

CHAPTER 30

Only the weekend to go and they would all be back at school. As he walked through the streets delivering the ironing for his mother, Connor was surprised how many people knew about his success at the exhibition. He was greeted with all sorts of compliments.

"That harebell picture was wonderful, Connor, so lifelike."

"That picture of your Ma was lovely Connor. It brought a lump to my throat. I bet she's so proud."

"However did you manage to paint all those wee fishermen on the quay laddie? I could almost smell the fish." And so it went on down the street. Connor's head was buzzing and his face aching with the perpetual smile of thanks. Of course these kind people didn't realise that his parents had not been to the exhibition and wouldn't know what they were talking about.

The last stop was the Big House. He went round the back as usual and Mrs Hubbard let him in.

"Mr Hughes would like to see you Connor," she said. "You're to go straight to the studio. And well done with your pictures!"

He made his way to the studio. Mr Hughes was sitting on the old saggy sofa that faced out into the wild garden.

"Come and sit down Connor. Would you like lemonade?"

Connor accepted the icy glass which was handed to him and sipped apprehensively. Mr Hughes looked very serious.

"I've been making enquiries, and contacted a friend of mine in the medical profession. I told him about you, I hope you don't mind, and the problem you have with your leg."

Connor's breath was on hold as Mr Hughes continued.

"I asked him if anything could be done about it and he was surprised you hadn't already been informed.

Apparently there are several ways to treat the problem as well as an operation that will make your legs the same length." Connor's eyes flew wide and his mouth opened in surprise. Mr Hughes hurried on. "Of course you will have to be properly assessed, for the medics to decide on the best treatment. Which will mean several visits to the mainland hospital." Connor was speechless. Mr Hughes studied him to try to gauge his reaction. "Well, what do you think?"

Connor leant forward, eyes wide with shock, mouth open.

"I can't believe it. Why did no-one tell me before?" He whispered.

"Perhaps the Doctor on the island didn't know about the treatment. The thing is, we have to talk to your father… if you want to have it done."

Connor turned and looked up at Mr Hughes. His face was glowing, his bottom lip caught by his teeth as if trying to stop himself laughing.

"Want it done? It's like a dream come true!" Then he did laugh and he did cry, covering his face with his hands. Mr Hughes put his arm around him, confused and not knowing what to say. He looked up helplessly as Sasha walked through the door. She ran to Connor and knelt in front of him wrapping him in her arms and saying all sorts of soothing nonsense to calm him down.

As his sobs subsided she grabbed a kitchen roll from the work bench, tore off a strip and handed it to Connor to wipe his face.

"Sorry," he mumbled. "I seem to be doing a lot of this recently. It's just..."

"We do understand," Mrs Hughes assured him looking up at him with deep concern clouding her lovely eyes. "Everything is a bit overwhelming at the moment."

"Yeah," He gave a shaky laugh and scrubbed at his eyes again giving a big sigh, calmness restored.

"When is the best time to speak to your father and mother?" Mr Hughes asked.

"Evenings are best. He doesn't seem to be going out in the boat at the moment, but tonight and tomorrow night he'll be in the pub playing darts, so Saturday evening. He'll be in then. But I can't guarantee he'll be pleased with the news."

"Well, we have to try."

Connor felt quite sick at the thought, and couldn't finish his lemonade.

Mrs Hughes noticed. "You're very white all of a sudden. It's been a huge shock. I'll make you some tea. Just sit there quietly Connor. Shut your eyes if you want to."

Connor sat back on the sofa, his head spinning, tears seeping out between his closed eyelids. He didn't care anymore. He hadn't cried since he was five and he seemed to be making up for lost time at the moment. Years of heartache spilled down his cheeks.

***

Once at home he sketched out the portrait of his mother onto a canvas Mrs Hughes had given him. He would work at the studio in the evenings after school to finish it. He had also begun a portrait of Morag. Using his sketches, he'd drawn her as she was dancing, half turned away, her arms outstretched, her face raised to the sky, skirts swirling in the wind, hair flying. This he would work on at home and when finished, would keep in his room.

***

After lunch, he visited the cove. There was no message

from Morag, so he had a swim, his head full of new thoughts. What sort of treatment would he have to have? What about an operation? What would it be like to be able to run and join in the normal games with the other lads? How long will it all take? And will it be painful?

He spent the evening with Danny and when Danny's parents went out for the evening he told him what Mr Hughes had said. Danny was overjoyed.

"That's the best news ever pal!" he said slapping Connor on the back. "We'll soon have you in our football team. What d'you think your Dad will say?"

"Who knows? I tell you this, though Danny. If he won't let me have the treatment, I'll leave home."

"Don't blame you, but where would you go?"

"Haven't worked that out yet." Connor frowned.

They watched TV and guzzled crisps and popcorn till Danny's parents returned.

"Everything OK? Connor, we loved your paintings, especially the pastel of little Suzie. When did you do that?" Mrs Stewart asked.

"At the Barbecue, I made the original sketch then did it in pastel later."

"It was lovely."

"How many did you sell in the end?" Mr Stewart asked, taking off his shoes and putting on his slippers.

Connor sent a warning glare at Danny, not wanting to let anyone know how much they sold for.

"I managed to sell them all in the end," He stated simply.

"I'm not surprised; they were very good." Mrs Stewart cut in. "Better than some of the adults' work that was shown. Are you going to make a career of it?"

"I don't know yet," Connor could feel his colour rising.

"Better than fishing Connor." Mr Stewart grinned at him.

CHAPTER 31

Mrs McKenzie made Connor try on his school clothes on Saturday morning. She shook her head.

"They won't do. Whatever have you been up to this holiday! You're bursting out of everything! Your shoulders are so wide, you can't do up your shirts properly and your trousers look like long shorts! We'll have to go into Gaelcreags and buy some new."

"Can we afford it?" Connor asked anxiously.

"I've saved my ironing money. I had an idea you'd be putting on a growth spurt."

"We could always use my painting money," Connor suggested.

"Never Connor. That money's yours. You earned it. Don't fret, we'll manage very well."

They set off to catch the bus. Mrs McKenzie had no intention of walking the cliff path.

There was only one shop in Gaelcreags that sold the school uniform and they always had plenty. Connor was in and out of the changing cubicle trying on shirts and trousers to get the exact fit. Then Mrs McKenzie insisted he have a weatherproof jacket and a new rucksack for his books.

Connor still had some money left over from his visit on Thursday so they browsed the Art shop, Connor treating himself to a set of pastels.

"I can give Mrs Hughes's pastels back now." He smiled happily.

"We'll have lunch in 'Madeleine's'," Mrs McKenzie said. "And you can order what you like."

"Wow Mum, that's a real treat!" Connor exclaimed.

"And then you can have a haircut."

Connor's smile vanished, "I hate having my hair cut!"

"You can't go back to school like that, you look like a girl."

They found a table in the window and studied the

144

menu.

"I wanted to do something a bit special for you," Mrs McKenzie said. "It's not been easy this holiday and we've had our differences, but I want you to know I'm proud of your achievement with your painting and I'm pleased to see you growing up and knowing your own mind. It's not only your body that's got stronger, I can see that you have developed as a person. You're not the meek little mouse you used to be." She grasped Connor's hand and gave it a squeeze. "And I'm glad. Now what do you want to eat?"

Connor didn't know how to reply to this amazing speech by his Mum. His cheeks were very pink and his eyes very bright when he mumbled.

"Thanks Mum." He paused. "Can I have the 'All Day Breakfast'?"

"Is that all you want?"

"It's got everything I like; then can I have some gateaux?"

"You're a funny lad at times," Mrs McKenzie chuckled. "I'm having steak! This is our celebration!"

Later, they found a suitable Barber shop and Connor submitted to the scissors first saying "Not too short please."

He had to admit when it was over that he did look better for the haircut. The Barber had cut the sides fairly short but only trimmed the curls on top. Connor looked 'cool'.

They caught the bus home to Carrickquays loaded with bags and feeling very pleased with themselves. It had been a long time since Connor and his Mum had had such a great time together. He couldn't remember when it had stopped, probably when money became short with the gradual decline in the fishing. His father, always a man of few words, seemed to have shut down completely, even with his wife, especially when she began to take in ironing. Connor reckoned it was his father's pride again and

145

wondered, not for the first time, how his Dad would react to what Mr Hughes had to say on Sunday evening.

***

Connor went down to the cove to see if there was a message from Morag on Sunday afternoon, but there was still no news. He felt very uneasy.

The sky glowered down at him. Clouds boiling up and rolling towards him over the sea. The waves edged with white. If a tidal wave began to gather right now, he thought, the island wouldn't stand a chance.

Morag had said something about the high spring tides that swept half way up the cliffs in September, when the moon was full. That was only two weeks off. They'd have to start making the beacon. He gathered up some dry driftwood and placed it in a heap at the top of the steps, sheltered from the wind which was beginning to howl across the beach. Then made his way home.

Connor decided to make himself scarce after tea. So he went round to Danny who was just going over to keep Rory company while he baby-sat his little sister. Rory's Mum and Dad had gone out for a meal to celebrate their wedding anniversary. Danny and Connor walked round together, Connor telling Danny what was going on at home and mentioning the beacon.

"We'll start on that tomorrow night," Danny said. "I wonder why Morag hasn't been in touch though."

"Maybe her uncle's still watching her. We've got about two weeks before the really high tides. I reckon that's when her uncle will make his move."

CHAPTER 32

"Mr Hughes came to see me last night." Connor's Dad spoke slowly as if the words were difficult to get out. Connor held his breath, bracing himself for the row to come. "He seems like a reasonable man, clever of course, but easy to get on with. He talked about some treatment you could have for your leg that would cure that limp of yours. We wouldn't have to pay for it either."

Connor heaved a huge sigh of relief. "He told me about it, said he'd come to talk to you."

"Well what do you think? You could join me on the boat then." Connor froze, he should have realised his Dad would expect that.

"It'll take time," Connor said hesitating. "We don't know what treatment would be best. There are a few options."

"Mr Hughes explained all that. It might take a year or so. He said he didn't mind taking you back and fore to the mainland for your appointments. He hasn't got a proper job, so he can afford the time. Well?"

"Dad, obviously I want to do it. It's like a dream come true for me."

"And the boat?"

"Let's see how good a job they do on my leg first."

Mr McKenzie stared thoughtfully at his son before going back to his paper.

***

The boys trudged up to the cliff top as the sun was dipping down to the west. Great flamingo feathers of cloud fanned out across the pale turquoise sky. The sea was tranquil and flat, a silver and blue expanse, shot through with pathways of apricot, orange and gold.

147

They gathered the driftwood that Connor had collected and piled it into the metal basket that had last been lit to welcome in the new millennium. The tide had receded so they climbed down once more and collected up a few more branches and heaped them up beside the basket. Then sat in friendly silence watching the changing colours of the sky.

"Did Mr Hughes talk to your Dad?" Danny asked Connor.

"Yep, and he took it really well. Thought Mr Hughes a 'reasonable man'. The thing is he now expects me to join him on the boat."

Danny gave a short chuckle. "There might be no boat by the time you finish the treatment. Rory's Dad is thinking of pulling out and looking for work elsewhere. There's only Ewan's Dad and Sam MacDonald and he's not as fit as he once was."

"That's probably why Dad wants me to join them... What's that out there?" Connor scrambled to his feet pointing. "Come on, I think it's Morag."

The boys hurried to the steps and made their way down to the beach. By the time they reached the sand, Morag was walking up the beach towards them carrying a large bundle in her arms.

"Where have you been?"

"What have you got there?" The boys chorused.

Morag dumped the bundle into Connor's arms. "It's the other Selkie cloak. I haven't been able to get away. My father and mother have had to go away for a few days. There is an emergency gathering of all the leaders of sea creatures. Something to do with sea temperature, I don't understand it, but my father has asked my uncle to look after me because he doesn't believe I will stay with my brothers and sisters. So I think that my uncle will make his move soon, while they are away."

"Do you think your uncle has said something to your

father about us?" Connor asked frowning.

"Oh no. If anything he's just hinted, but I think they are worried that if I stray, I'll disappear like my sister."

"Do you know what day the wave will come?" Danny cut in. "We've built the beacon. In case it's needed. Just hope it doesn't rain and make the wood wet. We need to know the day, 'Cos we're back to school tomorrow. And we can't do anything without Shelly's cloak either." Danny was uneasy, wondering if they were going to be needed and if their plan would work.

Morag turned to Connor. "I'm not sure of your days and months."

"I'll show you. We'd better go into the cave, the light is fading and we can't see properly now."

Morag lit up the cave and brought the notebook to Connor. They sat side by side on the rock and Connor patiently explained the months of the year using the Spring and Neap tides as examples. Morag grasped the information immediately. He then went back to the days of the week he had written out for her before then rewrote them adding the dates. He showed her where they were at the moment and continued into September.

Morag stared thoughtfully. "The High tides start about here." She pointed to the third of September. "He might make his move then. So I must find her cloak very soon."

"How long will it take me to reach Sula Sgeir and back wearing the Selkie cloak if I'm needed?" Connor asked, a worried frown creasing his forehead.

"Not as long as a man swimming. From here, it would not take long. As long as the sun moves from here to here." She drew a picture in the shingle of the sun setting, very low on the horizon, then changed it to show the sun disappearing below the sea.

"That's not very long," said Connor. "Only about an hour, but Sula Sgeir is forty kilometres away"

Morag laughed. "Selkies swim very fast! Didn't you

notice when you wore my cloak?"

"I didn't realise they could swim that fast, but anyway, I can't do anything until I have Shelly's cloak as well."

"I know. I've thought and thought about it. My uncle said he'd hide it somewhere where I would never find it. As if I'd be unable to think of the place."

"Perhaps you'll have to ask your bird friends," Danny suggested. "They helped you find your sister."

Morag smiled. "I'll do that, good idea!"

"And Morag," Connor chipped in. "Ask them if they've seen your uncle anywhere unusual. As he's the one who hid the cloak."

"I will. That's a good idea too."

"We're at school tomorrow so we'll have to meet up in the evening." Danny reminded them.

CHAPTER 33

The weather reflected the gloom felt by the students of the Island Academy as they all returned to school. The clouds were low and glowering and a thin wind whistled in their ears as Danny and Connor, and the other students from Carrickquays waited for the bus.

But things had changed for Connor during the holidays. He was healthier and stronger with a steady confidence shining in his eyes. Last term he had viewed himself as a lonely cripple with no future. He returned to school a successful artist with good friends and adults that believed in him, and although the immediate future was one of mystery and perhaps danger, he believed his long-term future was very bright indeed.

Everyone noticed the difference.

"Great haircut Connor," one girl remarked smiling.

"You been training over the holiday?" One of the older lads asked. "You look amazing!"

"Where d'you get that tan? Somewhere exotic?" another commented.

Connor felt six-foot-tall and suddenly the limp didn't matter.

Mr Thompson was their form tutor for the year and had been to the exhibition.

"Connor that was fine work you produced. Who taught you to use pastels and acrylics?" Connor told him about Mr and Mrs Hughes.

"I've heard of them. I've read one of Mr Hughes' books and she's famous in the world of fashion. I had no idea they lived on the island."

"They keep themselves very much to themselves," Connor said. "They hardly ever go into the village. It was just accident that Mr Hughes saw me drawing and invited me up to the house."

"I'm pleased for you. Well done. And is this your

chosen career now?"

Connor nodded emphatically. "Yes, it's what I really want to do."

***

The first week of school flew by with the students getting used to their new timetables, new text books to study and new rooms to study in, as well as catching up with old friends they hadn't seen for the whole of the Summer break.

Connor was spending his evenings in the studio working on the acrylic painting of his mother for her birthday which was the twenty fourth of August. He thought she would like it but was a bit apprehensive as to how his father would react.

He was also working on a series of paintings capturing the sea, the sky and the cliffs in different moods. Connor lost himself in these when he was painting, as if he was absorbed into the landscape he was creating, and was always a bit dazed when he stopped as if he really had been somewhere else. Mrs Hughes loved to watch him, as if the life that shone from his face was being channelled into the painting itself, which then became vibrant and living in turn.

One evening during a break in painting, Mr Hughes came in carrying a piece of paper.

"I've just received this email from a friend of mine in Edinburgh. It's a bit convoluted but I'll try and simplify it. A friend of his was on a tour of these islands during the Summer, and he bought two paintings from a local Art exhibition to hang in his lounge."

Connor looked up at that. "When my friend saw them, he was so struck by them that he wanted to find out who the Artist was. But all that he could discover was that the initials were C.M. and the exhibition was held at Gaelcreags. So, knowing that I lived near, he has asked me to find out the name of the Artist and for that person to get in touch with him." Mr Hughes was almost laughing. "Now who could that be Connor McKenzie?"

Connor's eyes were shining and he was grinning broadly. "Who is this man?" He asked.

"He owns a very prestigious gallery in Edinburgh and is very keen on having one section of the gallery for up and coming Artists. I'll give him a ring, assuming you're interested of course." He smiled broadly.

"Is that Maurice, Thomas?" Mrs Hughes asked.

"It is indeed Sasha." She raised her eyebrows and looked sideways at Connor. "That is amazing!"

"Sounds like it's a pretty good thing to happen?" Connor was a bit puzzled.

"The best Connor, the best!"

Mr Hughes returned just before Connor was setting off for home, his mother's painting wrapped in pretty wrapping paper.

"Well, Maurice is delighted I've found you so quickly and he wants to meet you and see the rest of your work, including your sketch books. I haven't told him your age Connor."

"Will it put him off?"

"I doubt it. To be honest, I just want to see the look on his face when he meets you." Mr Hughes had a gleeful glint in his eyes.

But then Connor stopped and a frown clouded his face. "I'm at school now. I can't just take time off."

"I'm sure it won't be a problem Connor. I'll explain everything in a letter to the Head Teacher."

"What about my Dad?"

"We'll face that when the time comes."

"If the Head says I can go, I'm going to go, even if Dad says no." His head was high and determination was written in every line of his body.

Sasha put her arm around his shoulder and looked up at him. "You have changed so much in six short weeks Connor."

CHAPTER 34

Connor presented his mother with the painting at breakfast time the next day. She was wordless. Her hand flew to her mouth as if to hold back the tears that Connor could see gathering in her eyes. Not given to elaborate shows of emotion, he was surprised when she held out her arms to him and drew him into a huge hug.

"My goodness," she exclaimed sniffing back the tears. "You're taller than me now! That is a lovely present Connor." She released him and held the picture at arm's length. "You are talented aren't you? Who would have thought it? I don't even mind that you've caught me doing the ironing... it's... beautiful!"

Connor's Dad entered at that moment and Connor's heart missed a beat. What would he say?

"What's that you've got there Mary?"

She turned the picture towards him and held it steady her mouth in a tight line. He stared in silence for what seemed an age and Connor could swear he saw his father's face soften as he gazed at the portrait of his wife.

"He's caught you just right Mary! Very nice Connor." Connor thought his heart would leap out of his throat. He wanted to give his Dad a great big bear hug but knew it would not be appreciated. So just gave his Dad a bemused smile.

***

Halfway through Monday morning, Connor was summoned to the Head's office. Everyone stared at him wide-eyed, wondering what it was all about, as he rose from his seat to leave the room. Although Connor knew, it didn't stop the butterflies playing havoc with his stomach. His mouth was dry when he knocked at the Head's door and his hands were sweaty and trembling slightly. He hoped Mr Frobisher, the Head, wouldn't notice.

The office was light, and decorated in neutral colours. The Head's desk free of clutter, the atmosphere business-like. Mr Frobisher was an imposing figure. His sparse gingery hair was very neat exposing a nut-brown dome. He had deep blue eyes which seemed to see right through you, so lying to the Head was always difficult. He smiled rarely but was known for his fairness, and understanding.

"Come in Connor, take a seat. I expect you know what this is all about." Connor nodded wordlessly. "I know of Mr Hughes, of course, I have a couple of his books. His letter is quite comprehensive as to the situation, but I would like to hear from you. How did you meet up?"

Connor cleared his throat and related all the events that had taken place during the holidays.

"I'm very pleased for you Connor. Mr Thompson, your year tutor, has informed me about your talent for painting and drawing. The thing that puzzles me is why Mr Hughes is writing to me and not your father."

Connor took a deep breath, his fingers which were clenched together showed white knuckles. This did not go unnoticed by Mr Frobisher.

Connor cleared his throat once more. "I haven't mentioned it to my father yet." His head was up as he looked steadily at Mr Frobisher.

The Head raised his eyebrows and tilted his head on one side. "Go on."

"My father is dead against my drawing and painting. He sees it as unmanly. He wanted me to follow him on the boat, but because of my leg, it would be impossible."

"I see." There was a long silence. "I cannot give you permission without the consent of your parents."

"Oh," Connor said hurriedly. "I am going to tell him. I wanted to know if I could have time off first." The Head was still very thoughtful as he studied Connor's face. The

156

boy had grown up over the holidays. He had physically developed and looked healthy and strong, not the weak lad of last term. The Head had always felt secretly sorry for Connor, but this boy, although nervous in the Head's presence, had somehow developed an inner strength and determination. The Head could see it in his eyes.

"And is this something you want to make of your life? Is drawing and painting what you really want to do?"

Connor's eyes blazed with such intensity and passion, the Head's eyes widened and he smiled, remembering the passionate desire he had had for teaching when he was young.

"Well Connor, I have no problem with you following this path and I will support you every step of the way, but I will need to talk to your father. I will write a note for you to take to him tonight. You can collect it from my secretary after school." They stood up and Mr Frobisher leant forward holding out his hand for Connor to shake which he did, his face breaking into a dazzling smile of delight.

He told Danny everything as they munched their packed lunches together managing to evade the questions of their curious class mates.

"Do you think your Dad will let you go?"

"I'm beginning to think he might. He was different somehow when he saw the painting I gave to Mum on her birthday."

"Any news from Morag?"

"No. We really need that cloak of Shelly's. Time's running out. The tides are building."

"Maybe he will make his move later. Morag was only guessing it would be the third."

"Umm, maybe there'll be a message tonight." The bell went for the beginning of afternoon school. They drifted off to their next lesson.

157

***

Connor collected the letter and thrust it in his bag as they all clambered on the bus to return to Carrickquays. He gave it to his Dad as they were sitting eating their tea.

After he'd read it through he asked, "What's this all about then? You wanting time off from school?"

"Yes Dad. I'll need two or three days. An Edinburgh gallery is interested in my paintings and wants to meet me and see the rest of my work."

"But you're just a boy!"

"He doesn't know that, he's only seen my paintings."

"You'll have to let him go Andrew," his mother spoke up. "You've seen for yourself how clever he is with the paints. It could be a real chance for him." Mr McKenzie eyed his wife and sighed.

"He's won you over with that picture of his. What about the boat... when you get your leg fixed?" He stared intently at Connor. "It's not going to happen is it Connor? Even with a good leg you don't want to follow your father and become a fisherman."

Connor faced him boldly. "No Dad I don't. I want to be a painter."

Mr Mckenzie shrugged defeated shoulders. "Well, I can't see it lasting much longer for me. So all I can do is let you follow your own path and hope it takes you where you want to go. I won't stand in your way lad." They finished their meal each wrapped in their own thoughts.

CHAPTER 35

Connor's father spent a long time talking to the Head Master.

"Well that Head Master of yours seems to put a lot of store by your painting Connor," he said at the tea table. "I told him I'd come round to the idea and thought you should give it a try. There's no future in fishing that's for sure."

It was then Connor decided to share an idea that had been flitting in and out of his mind ever since the day he had met Danny in the shop when it was crowded out with tourists.

"Dad, I was thinking, there are more and more tourists visiting the islands these days. They love going on fishing trips or just touring the islands by boat. Have you thought about that? Apparently you can make a lot of money from it and you wouldn't necessarily go night fishing."

"That would be lovely Andrew. You could choose your times," his mother added.

"You'd be so good at it Dad. You know these waters and the fishing grounds so well." A gleam had come into his father's eyes, but he just mumbled a reply.

When tea was over Mr McKenzie left the table abruptly.

"I'm off out for a bit."

"Probably going to the pub," said Connor's mother when he had left. "That was a good idea of yours about the tourists, I hope he takes it up. He's getting a bit old for these night fishing trips."

But Mr McKenzie was not going to the pub. He walked through the village and up the hill to the Big House.

Mr and Mrs Hughes were surprised, but welcomed him in warmly. He stayed for over an hour talking about Connor's prospects in the Art world. They took him through to the studio and showed him all the work Connor had been doing. The brilliant acrylic landscapes capturing the changing moods of the sea, the fragile delicate watercolours of the island's plants, the gentle, tender pastels of his friends caught and sketched when they weren't looking. There was another of Mrs Mckenzie dozing in the sunshine in her chair, head on one side. A tendril of hair had escaped from her bun and fell almost girlishly over her shoulder.

Mr Mckenzie's cheeks were wet with tears as he gazed in awe.

"My! That's just how she looked when I first met her. A bonny young thing of twenty and I so much older, couldn't believe she could be interested in an old fisherman like me." He continued to stare at the pastel. "We'd been married a long time," he reminisced. "Thought we'd never have children. Then Connor came along and he was so marred, it broke my heart. Now look at what he can do! Who'd have thought it?" He turned to Mr Hughes. "You've been good to my son. You've been to him what I should have been, I can see that now. You encouraged him to be what he was meant to be. I was wrong to try to force him into a way of life that he wasn't cut out for. I want you to know I'm grateful." He held out his hand and Mr Hughes shook it, a delighted smile on his face.

"Let's hope things work out well for him on our trip to Edinburgh."

"You have my best wishes. Both of you," Mr McKenzie said nodding in Sasha's direction. "I'd best be off."

***

Connor had too much homework that night to go up to the Big House or he would have met with his Dad, but he did have time to go down to the cove to see if there was a

160

message from Morag.

The tide was racing up the beach in a frenzy as if hungry to devour the rocks and sand. It swirled around his feet nearly pulling him over as he made his way to the cave. There was no message and no extra cloak. Connor was beginning to be anxious, there was only a week left. Whatever was Morag up to?

***

Morag had visited every cave and rocky islet she could think of, to no avail. So she turned to her friends the gulls and gannets and asked them if they had seen her uncle anywhere unusual. They had all said no. He had only been seen in the usual places; out at sea diving for eels and flatfish, basking on the rocky islets, visiting his relatives at Sule Skerry and chasing the fishing boats for unwanted live fish.

Morag had been to all those places except her home island of Sule Skerry. When she found out her uncle had visited when her parents were away she became suspicious. 'The last place to look', he had said, well she would never have thought of searching the island of Sule Skerry. She sped off as fast as she could go while her uncle was out chasing the boats again.

She reached the island and waited until her brothers and sisters slid into the water, off on a hunting trip, leaping and diving through the foamy waves. Casting off her cloak she clambered up the rocks and looked around, wondering where Shelly's cloak might be hidden. The island was very small, but even so it took her a long time to look in every cave and cranny. It had to be somewhere that would be difficult to see by a casual observer. As soon as she heard her siblings returning she slipped into the sea. She didn't want them telling her uncle she'd been to see them. He might become suspicious and move the cloak. Morag decided she would return again the next day convinced that it was hidden on her home island.

Morag could not remember the days of the week very well without seeing it written down, but she was aware that the moon was growing rounder each night and when there were no clouds to hide it, it's huge orange face sent a golden path across the sea.

She returned once more to the island and gazed around her. Where had she not searched? She was staring at the tall lighthouse that stood looking out over the great, grey ocean. Suddenly, she was racing towards it. The stout door at the bottom of the tower was never locked as humans rarely visited and if they did they wouldn't be interested in the lighthouse. She ran up the twisting stairs, till she came out at the top where the light whirled round and round sending out a great shaft of light, so passing ships would not founder on the craggy rocks. Tucked away under the light itself was her sister's cloak. She dragged it out and hugged it to her.

As she gazed out over the sea, she could see her brothers and sisters returning, but also behind them she could see her uncle, ploughing through the waves like a speed boat. She gathered the cloak and sped down the stairs slamming the door she raced down to the rocks. An old Selkie was basking in the intermittent sunshine. She spoke to him quickly.

"Venerable friend can you do something for me of great importance and secrecy?"

The old Selkie looked at her. "Anything for you Princess."

"Can you take this bundle to Dernvoe and hide it at the back of the cave there and not tell a soul?" she whispered.

The wise eyes sparkled and he took the bundle in his

162

mouth and dived silently under the waves.

Morag rose and went to meet her brothers and sisters who were overjoyed to see her. They hugged and chatted sharing news. Morag boasting about the beauties of her uncle's cave and saying how much she missed them all, but mostly listening to their tales and stories. They all turned to stare as their uncle climbed the rocks towards them.

"Morag I was wondering where you had got to."

"Uncle, it has been so long since I spent time with my brothers and sisters. I had to come and see them. I could wait no longer. I'm sorry if I worried you."

"You must not wander off without telling me where you are going. Remember the fate of your sister."

It was a warning that carried a weight of meaning to Morag. He was threatening her, though her family would not realise it.

"We must return at once. Your father has put me in charge of you."

"Yes uncle," Morag replied meekly. She embraced her family one by one and left, following her Uncle, relieved that he had suspected nothing.

When Morag woke the next morning she was unable to find her cloak. The truth dawned on her. She stormed into her uncle's chamber.

"What have you done with my cloak?"

"It's quite safe my dear, only you won't be needing it until the day of the Wave, and the time is drawing very near now, so you won't have long to wait, as long as you do as you are told."

CHAPTER 36

Friday evening was spent at the studio selecting which paintings to take to the gallery. Mrs Hughes was helping Connor make his choices when Mr Hughes joined them.

"That's all settled then. I've just been speaking to Maurice. He is able to see us on the fourth of September, then he's off to the States for a few weeks. We'll have to leave early on the third. It takes about eight hours to drive there. We'll pick you up at about six o'clock Connor, don't sleep in."

"I might not get to sleep at all that night," Connor grinned, then stopped, frowning. He rubbed his forehead.

"Did you say the third?" He asked.

"Yes, it's this Monday, why?"

"I can't go on the third. There's something I have to do here." Connor was as white as a sheet.

"Surely you can do it another day? It's all arranged. This is important Connor."

"I know," he exclaimed fiercely, his fists clenched.

Mrs Hughes went to him and put her hand on his shoulder. "What is it Connor?" He was obviously distressed.

He looked down biting his lips and rubbing his forehead again. Then looked up at them with appeal in his eyes as if begging them to understand.

"I'm sorry, I can't tell you, but I really can't go."

Mr Hughes sat down heavily on one of chairs that were scattered about the studio.

"Well, I know Maurice will be disappointed at not meeting you, but I can still take your paintings. If you'd like me to do that."

"Would you? I'm so sorry to let you down." Mr Hughes heaved a great sigh of disappointment.

"Yes, I can't let Maurice down after going to all this trouble. Have you finished choosing the work you want to show him?" Connor looked at Mrs Hughes.

164

"Yes Thomas we've covered a whole range of subjects and different media. We'll wrap them and put them in the boot of the car ready for Monday." She pulled Connor into a hug. "I'm sure it will all work out for you," she said softly.

***

There was no message and no extra cloak in the cave on Saturday and it was with a leaden heart that he made his way to the beach early on Sunday morning but again there was nothing. Unless Morag was able to rescue her sister. If the cloak didn't arrive there was no way, he could save the island, and everything and everyone would be destroyed on Monday.

Connor returned to the cave on Sunday afternoon willing the cloak to be there or at least a message from Morag saying she had rescued Shelly herself. As he entered the mouth of the cave, he stumbled over something that was lying in a heap on the sand. He scrambled to his feet and picked up the bundle, spreading it out and seeing straight away that it was another Selkie cloak displaying a white shell shape high up near the collar. Shelly's cloak! He had to tell Danny that today was the day to rescue Shelly and he would need to be ready to light the beacon.

He raced from the cave, and immediately knew something was wrong. The sea was receding rapidly as if it was being sucked away by a powerful force. Far out towards the horizon the water was building slowly and forming a wave.

A huge gasp escaped Connor and he stumbled for the steps cursing his leg that refused to let him run. He had to tell Danny that he was going and that the tidal wave was already building. It wouldn't take long before everyone noticed what was happening and panic would break out.

165

He reached Danny's shop desperately trying to calm the shuddering breaths that rose up threatening to choke him. He forced his face to be calm as he walked into the shop and asked if Danny was about as it was his day off. Danny came into the shop through the back entrance and knew straight away that something was happening. He didn't say anything to his Dad just walked out with Connor into the street.

"It's happening isn't it?" He said taking Connor's arm.

Connor nodded. "Shelly's cloak was there this afternoon, but Danny... the Wave is coming."

"Blimey! What do you want me to do?" Danny went white.

"Everyone's going to panic when they see it coming, but if you could slip away in a couple of hours' time, and wait for me then you'll be there to light the beacon. I must go. The sooner I find Shelly the sooner the Wave will be stopped."

Danny clapped him on the back "Best of luck pal. I'll be there."

Connor sped as fast as he could, back to the cave. The Wave didn't seem to be growing that fast. He wondered if Morag was being deliberately slow to give them more time.

He grabbed both cloaks, tying Shelly's tightly around his waist. He had no idea where Sula Sgeir was but as soon as he reached the water, flung the other cloak around his shoulders and plunged beneath the waves, he knew immediately which way he should go.

At first it was easy to cleave through the water and he made great progress, swimming at top speed, but the nearer he got to the rising Wave he could feel himself slowing down and very soon he was struggling.

He dived deeper and for while was able to speed up but gradually the tug of the current pulled at him, slowing him down again. Connor struggled on, every now and then rising to the surface to take a great gulp of life-giving air.

166

He could feel Sula Sgeir drawing nearer. But it was still a long way off. The waves buffeted him so he dived once more, forcing himself forwards.

***

Back on the island the people began to notice what was happening and they all ran to their homes putting up their shutters and piling sandbags, if they had any, in front of their doors. Spare bags were shared out among their neighbours.

Some took to the boats and set off to the other side of the island away from the threatening Wave, others raced up the hill where Mr and Mrs Hughes opened up their house to everyone who asked for protection and they all waited in dread wondering when the wave would hit and why it was so slow in coming.

The reason of course was Morag. She had never made a wave of this magnitude before and it was taking all her energy to keep it going, so every now and then she had to stop and rest which meant the Wave faltered and diminished. Then when she regained her strength the Wave grew once more but it was quite a slow process. He uncle became angrier and angrier with her but there was nothing he could do except bluster and shout.

***

It took Connor two and a half hours to reach Sula Sgeir. He could hardly pull himself out of the water when he arrived, he was so exhausted. He stumbled and fell, banging his head. The sharp rocks scraped and scratched his limbs, but he was too worn out to notice. He limped across the rocks, the cloak dragging behind him as he called out Shelly's name in a croaky voice, searching for a cave that had an inlet of water running into it. He found it eventually and called Shelly's name more strongly. An answering cry greeted him.

"I've come from your sister Morag," he shouted. "I've got your Selkie cloak can you please come out I need to get back to save the island from your uncle."

A waif-like creature emerged from the mouth of the cave dressed in the same grey dress that Morag always wore. She was smaller than Morag and looked terrified.

"It's OK," said Connor. "I won't hurt you. I'm a friend of your sister."

"But you are human."

"Yes, I know I can't explain now, I'm in a hurry."

"My leg is tethered," she said indicating a thin cord made out of nylon fishing net that twisted about her ankle.

Connor had no idea what to do about that. He knew how tough the nylon was and he had no knife. The rocks were covered in barnacles and were prickly to walk over. He took the thin strand and began to rub it up and down the sharp peaks of the shells, pulling and stretching it at the same time. It took ages and he was almost crying with frustration when it began to fray. He renewed his efforts until at last the fibres separated and Shelly was free.

He undid her cloak from around his waist and threw it at her. "Put this on and go!" he said, "back to your brothers and sisters and tell them everything." Shelly didn't need him to tell her twice. She fastened the cloak and dived... gone in a flash.

Connor dragged himself over the rocks fastening the cloak and he too slid into the water.

CHAPTER 37

The Wave was drawing nearer to the island every minute as Danny raced up to the beacon. He'd taken a canister of paraffin from the shop to make sure the fire burned well, and a large bottle of lemonade to keep him company. Down in the village Mr and Mrs McKenzie were in a panic as they couldn't find Connor anywhere. Danny had told them truthfully he hadn't seen Connor since the early afternoon and had no idea where he was. Which was true as he could be anywhere in the sea at that moment.

Connor had set off at half past two or there abouts, so Danny reckoned he would be back by half past six at the latest. But of course Danny had no idea of the strength of the currents tugging at Connor and slowing him down. He settled on the grass to wait, watching the dark line of the Wave growing taller and bit by bit moving closer. By seven o'clock Danny was seriously worried.

"Where are you Connor?" he muttered. "The time's running out. Come on you've got to get here."

At ten to eight the Wave could be seen towering into the sky, blotting out the setting sun and casting a huge shadow before it. The white glittering frill of foam looked like hungry teeth to Danny who knew he'd be the first islander to go, as it would sweep up over the clifftop carrying Danny and the beacon with it.

As he looked, something else was bobbing towards the shore fighting the current that was sucking the water back from the sand and trying to draw it up into the Wave. Danny stood up peering through the gloomy twilight. It was a seal… it was Connor! Danny waited till Connor rose to his feet dropping the cloak he waved at Danny, staggered a few paces then collapsed on the sand.

It took all Danny's strength of will to stay where he was and light the fire. As soon as it was blazing he ran down the steps and across the beach till he reached his friend.

169

He turned him over gently. Connor's chest was heaving, sucking in air like a bellows. He was icy cold and shivering, his teeth chattering.

Danny stripped off his own jacket and wrapped it round his friend and lifted him to his feet. Their long shadows went before them up the shore, everything was bathed in a rosy, golden light. It was then that Danny realised, the Wave had gone and the setting sun was sending warm shafts of light across the landscape. In the distance he could hear people cheering.

"You've done it pal! You've saved the island. The Wave has gone. We're safe!"

Connor gave a weak smile. "I'm glad," he whispered.

Danny had to carry him up the steps. He had no energy left and all his limbs were trembling. Danny laid him down close to the brazier so he could feel the warmth and dry out. He piled on more wood to keep it going longer. Connor began to thaw out.

"I'm dying for a drink of something," he muttered, licking his dry, salty lips.

"It just so happens," said Danny, who brought out from behind a clump of grass the large bottle of fizzy lemonade. "Compliments of Stewart's Groceries." He passed the bottle to Connor who was sitting up now. He took a long drink.

They waited a while until Connor regained some of his strength. Night had fallen but it wasn't dark as a huge orange Harvest moon beamed down on them. There was the sound of voices coming up the path and Mr Stewart and Mr McKenzie appeared.

"Is that you Danny?" Mr Stewart called.

"Yeah Dad, it's me and Connor."

"What on earth are you doing up here? We've been going out of our minds with worry!" Mr Stewart was angry. "And why light the beacon?"

"We thought we ought to warn the other islands that

170

the Wave was coming." Danny lied expertly, glad the darkness hid his blushes.

"Well," his anger abated somewhat, "that was very thoughtful of you... but come down to the village now. There's a bit of a celebration going on."

The boys got up. Mr Stewart flung his arm around Danny's shoulders as they walked back to the village.

Mr McKenzie grabbed Connor and held him close. "I'm glad you're safe," he mumbled. They walked slowly down the hill.

The village was certainly celebrating, with food cooked over a bonfire on the quayside, a Ceilidh band playing dance tunes and people dancing and whooping with joy. The boys hadn't seen anything like it since New Year's eve, but neither had the energy to join in.

"I'm off to bed," Connor whispered to Danny. "I'm absolutely shattered."

"I'm not surprised pal. See you tomorrow."

***

There was no sign of his Mum, but Connor was too tired to worry about it. He washed thoroughly when he got in, until all the salt was off his skin and out of his hair. He was surprised to see how many scratches and bruises he had collected. He set his alarm for five thirty rolled himself in his duvet and slept deeply until the alarm rang in the morning.

When Mr McKenzie told his wife Connor was safe, she ran home and walked softly up the stairs. Heaving a huge sigh, she stood by Connor's bed looking down at her sleeping son. Knowing that there was a mystery here that she couldn't fathom.

Connor rose and dressed quietly so as not to wake his father and mother and made his way downstairs. He left a

171

note for his Mum and Dad and went out through the back door. He waited at the side of the road until he saw the headlights of a powerful car coming down the hill towards him. He stepped out into the road waving his arms. The car stopped and Mr Hughes leaned out of the window.

"Changed your mind?" He asked smiling. "Hop in."

Connor jumped in and settled himself comfortably in the passenger seat.

Mr Hughes looked curiously at Connor for a moment taking in scratches and bruises on his arms and one high up on his forehead beneath his curls.

"You look a bit beaten up Connor. Will you tell me what's been going on?"

"It's nothing serious. I didn't even know I had them till last night."

"I expect you can do with some more sleep. You look exhausted. We'll talk later."

Connor settled further down into his seat and closed his eyes. The soft purring of the engine lulled him to sleep.

CHAPTER 38

Connor slept through both ferry journeys, but woke for a while once they were on the mainland. Then fell asleep once more until they pulled into a service station for breakfast. Connor was ravenous and devoured a fried breakfast accompanied by toast and two mugs of tea.

Mr Hughes watched him in amusement. "When did you last eat?" he teased.

Connor grinned, his cheeks bulging, and Mr Hughes was glad to see some of the sparkle return to Connor's eyes.

"I'm very grateful to you," Connor said, waving the remains of the toast in the air. "I will try to pay you back."

"Connor just seeing your talent develop is payment enough for me. I'm grateful to you. You have filled a very real gap in our lives. We were unable to have children of our own and you came along and it's been a privilege to be able to do for you, what I would have done for a son of my own. Now tell me where were you when we were threatened by that tidal wave? I expected you to bring your parents up to the Big House, but apparently you were nowhere to be found and they were frantic with worry."

Connor's colour rose in his cheeks and he looked down at his empty plate, then raised his head and fixed Mr Hughes with his piercingly blue gaze.

"Can we talk in the car?"

"Fine by me. I take it you've finished?"

Connor nodded. "Thank you."

Once on the road again Connor began his story.

"Danny is the only person who knows about this. We needed his help."

"We?"

"Morag and me. I'd better start at the beginning."

"Morag's the girl you sketched on the beach?"

"That's right."

173

Connor related the whole tale never once checking Mr Hughes' face to see if he believed him or not. Every detail was etched into his mind and in talking it out found himself re-living the events.

When he had finished, Connor sneaked a sideways look at Mr Hughes

"You saved the island. No wonder you're… beaten up. And you thought this was all going to happen today and that's why you said you couldn't come, there was something you had to do." He chuckled. "You are a remarkable young man, Connor. I understand now why the wave never reached the island, Morag knew it was safe to stop, because she saw the lighted beacon. That's what Danny was doing."

"Yeah, I'm glad it's over though."

"What will happen to Morag's uncle now?"

"I have no idea. I hope Morag can meet up with us. I've got to return the cloak. The thing is, Morag started everything off for me. She wasn't disappointed that I couldn't do running and stuff she invited me into her world and it was there, in the sea, that I had the first taste of what it was like to be normal. I was free of my disability. I was determined to be the best swimmer ever."

"Well it seems you've achieved that, and the Art?"

Connor gave him that direct brilliant gaze again. "That was you. Again, for the first time ever it made me realise I didn't have to be a useless person. I could make my life out of something I could do, that didn't demand two equal legs."

"And college?"

"I'd like to go. If I sell my paintings, I could pay for it."

"There are scholarships Connor, but we can talk about that when we see Maurice Cavendish. Now get some more rest we've a long way to go and you still look washed out."

***

They arrived at half past two in the afternoon. Mr Hughes drove straight to their hotel. He had booked two rooms with en suite bathrooms and showers.

Connor was amazed, he had never experienced such luxury.

"If you don't mind Connor, I'm going to grab an hour's rest. Can you look after yourself?"

"No problem," he smiled, pulling out his sketchbook and making for the window.

The view was fascinating. So many roofs and angles and straight lines. The buildings were tall, nearly all of them three or four storeys high, and weathered, mottled browns and greys. He could see the tall, dark spire of a church and in the distance the formidable castle crowning the distant hill.

Time flew. Connor's intense concentration was broken when Mr Hughes knocked on his door.

"I think you ought to wash and brush up a bit before we go out. What clothes have you brought?"

Connor looked at Mr Hughes blankly. Who promptly burst out laughing.

"Oh Connor you are priceless! Although I don't suppose you had much time to think about it. You were rather busy. Have a shower, then we can go shopping."

They wandered through the ancient streets. Connor was bemused by the traffic and the number of shops displaying such a variety of wonderful things. In a department store they bought Connor two complete sets of clothes, one to change into before they had dinner in the hotel and another set for meeting Mr Cavendish the following day.

Over dinner Mr Hughes was aware of the glances of the other guests as they looked at Connor. He was certainly a picture of youthful health and well-being with his golden tan, bright blue eyes and caramel curls streaked by the sun. He was very striking to look at. He asked Connor what he thought of Edinburgh.

"It's very noisy and smells of petrol, but I like it I think. Some of the buildings are very beautiful, especially when you look up. The old carvings are still there. Everything feels, exciting and busy, and it, sort of, makes me feel like that too."

"Would you want to live here?"

"If there was somewhere quiet, out of the town maybe, it would be OK. It's a long way from Carrickquays."

"You've come a long way in six weeks Connor and not just from Carrickquays."

CHAPTER 39

They arrived at The Cavendish Gallery at eleven o'clock. They were ushered into Maurice Cavendish's office. He was a small, round, man wearing a suit and waistcoat and a broad jovial smile. He walked towards Mr Hughes holding out his hands in welcome.

"Thomas! So good to see you. It's been a long time." They shook hands and Mr Cavendish turned with a slightly puzzled frown to Connor. "And... who is this?" he asked brightly.

Mr Hughes introduced them. "Connor McKenzie, meet Maurice Cavendish." They shook hands, but the puzzled frown was still there. "The artist Maurice. You wanted to meet the artist."

The penny dropped. "Oh C.M. Connor McKenzie! Of course." He gaped in amazement, then, recovering quickly he smiled at Connor. "Well this is a surprise. Come, sit down we'll have some coffee. Did you bring any more examples of your work?"

Connor nodded. "They're in the car."

Mr Cavendish pressed a buzzer on his desk and a smartly dressed woman entered.

"Coffee please Anita, and could you arrange for Mr McKenzie's work to be brought up to the studio?" Mr Hughes handed Anita the car keys.

"Well, I can't pretend that this is something that has happened before. How old are you? And how long have you been painting? The ones I have seen are quite remarkable."

"I'm fourteen and I've been drawing and painting all my life."

"You haven't had any training or teaching?"

Connor glanced briefly at Mr Hughes who was sitting back relaxing, perfectly ay ease, enjoying the moment.

"Mrs Hughes has helped me during these holidays,

177

showed me how to use acrylics and pastel."

"Pastels too. Just these six weeks, you've not used acrylics or pastel before?"

"No, I couldn't afford them."

Mr Cavendish turned his attention to Mr Hughes. "That's why his work is so fresh, Thomas. No influence. Trust you to notice that." He was smiling broadly. "You always had a nose for talent."

The coffee was brought in at that point and set on the table between them.

"The paintings are in the studio, Mr Cavendish," said Anita.

They drank their coffee and the two men chatted about the various activities they were involved in. Then they all made their way up to the studio.

The paintings and drawings had been arranged around the walls, Connor's sketch books had been placed on the long, central table.

The acrylic landscapes gleamed in the bright light that shone through windows overhead, the colours glowed like jewels. They were the first to catch the eye. Mr Cavendish stood for a long time gazing at each in turn, then moved to study the pastel drawings. He exhaled slowly.

"Such a change in energy and emotion!" He seemed to be talking to himself as he studied the drawings. "These are so bold Connor, and exciting." He indicated the landscapes. "And these are so gentle and tender. This lady here?"

"My mother," Connor replied.

Mr Cavendish nodded, and moved on to look at the watercolour sketches. "Again that delicate touch, but so much detail. This meadow is delightful!"

"That's our garden." Mr Hughes commented.

"Ah yes, Sasha always loved the wild flowers."

Mr Cavendish moved over to look at the sketch books. He turned each page thoughtfully, stopping at the sketches

178

of Morag and the boys playing football.

"And you've never done life drawing?" Connor again shook his head. "But you obviously know how a body works. When did you do this?" He was looking at the pencil sketch of Edinburgh.

"I did it yesterday from our hotel window."

"Time to chat I think."

They went back downstairs and settled themselves on the comfortable sofas.

"Tell me all about yourself Connor and what you hope to achieve with your life. Where do your parents fit in?"

Connor took a deep breath and started at the beginning; the reason Art became important to him, his dream of going to college and wanting it to be his life, and the fact that his father had hoped he would be a fisherman and follow in his footsteps.

"I don't think it will do you any harm to go to college, But I'd hate you to lose that freshness and your unique way of seeing things."

"My parents can't afford to send me to college."

"That's not a problem, you can apply for a scholarship, and if you would like me to take some of your work to hang in my gallery. I could sell them for you."

Connor's eyes were shining. "Would you really?"

"I have no doubt at all that your paintings and drawings will sell. You will need to get the necessary qualifications at school of course, in order to go to college. You have another four years of education to get through. In the meantime, I will take any paintings you want to send my way, to hang in my 'Up and Coming Artists Gallery'. How does that suit you?"

"That suits me very well," Connor's face was beaming. "I can't thank you both enough!"

"I would like to keep the landscapes and the pastels for now. Do you have a bank account? I can pay any monies straight in for you." Connor didn't have his bank details on

179

him.

"I'll email them to you Maurice," Mr Hughes said. "Many thanks." They shook hands.

"My pleasure Thomas. You have a bright future young man," he said as he shook Connor by the hand.

The rest of the paintings and drawings were stacked carefully into the car and they drove back to the hotel.

CHAPTER 40

They spent the rest of the day visiting The City Art Centre which displayed historic and Contemporary Art and after lunch they wandered around the Royal Botanical Gardens as the weather was fine and sunny. Mr Hughes took Connor out to dinner in the evening, as a celebration and they talked about Connor's future and school work, which according to Connor wasn't very good.

***

They arrived back late in the afternoon at Carrickquays, on the Wednesday.

"I'll come down later and talk to your Dad," Mr Hughes said as he dropped Connor off at his house.

Connor pushed open the back door and walked into the kitchen.

His father put down the paper. "Well lad how did you get on?"

Connor was still trying to get used to his Dad's change of heart.

"Let the lad come in and sit Andrew. Do you want some tea love?"

"A cup of tea would be nice."

His mother bustled about boiling the kettle.

"Well?" his Dad said again, impatient now.

"The man at the gallery, Maurice Cavendish liked my work and has kept some to hang. He thinks they'll sell quite quickly."

"Well done boy!" His father exclaimed. "Mr Hughes said you were good." Connor couldn't stop grinning though tears threatened.

"Here drink this, you've had a long journey," his mother said, breaking the silence, handing him his tea.

"What else did they say?" This was the hard bit.

"They think I should try for Art College, but you won't have to pay, because I can get a scholarship, as well as have the money from any paintings I sell. It won't cost you a penny. Mr Hughes is coming down tonight to talk to you, if that's OK."

"I'll be pleased to see him. I have one or two things to talk to him about, myself. Now, tell us what was Edinburgh like. I've never been."

So as Mrs McKenzie set about laying the table and placing their evening meal before them, Connor related all he'd seen and done. The hotel, the shops, the Art gallery and the Botanical Gardens. He showed them his sketch of Edinburgh and tried to explain how he would depict it in paint. His face shining with enthusiasm as, for the first time, he was sharing his passion for painting with his parents.

When the meal was over, Connor went out to visit Danny. He wanted to make sure that they met up with Morag together, hopefully the following day, after school. Danny welcomed him in with a huge bear hug.

"What's been going on?" he asked. "Nobody said anything at school when you didn't show up. So I guessed the teachers knew all about it. Whatever it was."

"I'm sorry Danny, so much has been happening I didn't get a chance to tell you."

"Let's go up to my room." He grabbed two packets of crisps from the cupboard in the kitchen and they raced up the stairs.

"Mr Hughes managed to get me an interview with a friend of his who owns a gallery in Edinburgh. He saw a couple of my pictures from the island exhibition and was interested in meeting the artist. Of course he had no idea who had done them. I nearly didn't get to go though as we had to leave early on the third and I thought that's when the Wave would hit. So I told Mr Hughes I couldn't go."

182

"Wow!" Danny exclaimed. "I bet he wasn't happy with that."

"No he wasn't but he agreed to take the paintings anyway. It was the hardest thing I've ever done, saying I couldn't go and not being able to tell him why. Luckily for me the Wave hit early. And we saved the island between us!" They high-fived each other.

"So that's where you've been is it? Edinburgh? What was it like?"

So Connor told Danny everything that had happened including telling Mr Hughes all about Morag and the tidal wave.

"And he believed you?"

"I was a bit scratched and bruised after that mammoth swim even with the Selkie cloak on it was rough I can tell you."

"I noticed the scratches. He's some guy, that Mr Hughes! So you're going to be rich and famous. Put our island on the map!"

"And it's all down to you Danny."

"What d'you mean 'all down to me'. What did I do?"

"You gave me the poster advertising the exhibition. If you hadn't done that, I wouldn't have put any paintings in."

They fell about laughing.

"Seriously though I've got so many people to thank for believing in me, not just you, but Morag too and Mr and Mrs Hughes of course. I'll never forget our first meeting. He made me feel I could be a winner not a loser."

"What about your parents?"

"Well Mum came round first and said she was proud of me. She loved the portrait I gave her for her birthday. And Dad just seems to have melted. I think Mr Hughes convinced him that I could make a good living out of painting. So he's OK with it too."

"So what now? Life's going to be pretty dull with just

183

options to choose and exams to look forward to."

"We have to see Morag again to return the cloak, so I thought we should go down to the cove tomorrow after school. Hopefully we'll meet her."

"Do you think it might be the last time we see her, now her Dad knows about us?"

"I hope not!" Connor exclaimed in dismay. "We're such good friends!"

Danny's mouth twisted sideways and gave Connor a wry look. "Just wondering."

***

"Did Mr Hughes fill you in on the details about our trip to Edinburgh?" Connor asked at breakfast the next morning.

"He did that, and helped me write a letter to that Mr Cavendish, saying I approved of you hanging your paintings in his gallery. He'll take a cut of what they sell for, Connor. That's how these places work. He's promised to put a fair price on each one so you won't be out of pocket. I don't want you cheated lad."

"Thanks Dad. I don't think he will. He seemed a very fair man and, he's a friend of Mr Hughes."

"I had a few things to say to Mr Hughes myself."

"Oh what was that then?" Connor asked buttering himself some toast.

"I asked him if he could look after you over this operation to your leg. I can't write fancy letters to high-up Doctors and such and I don't think me or your Mum would be much good ferrying you to and from appointments. So I asked him if he would take it on."

"That was some 'ask' Dad! What did he say?" Connor's eyes were wide.

"He said he was going to ask me if he could, but he didn't want to offend me, that it would be a privilege to

184

help out in this way. He's a good man Connor. Had no children of their own. I think you've filled a gap in their lives."

"You don't mind Dad?"

"No, I've not been much of a Dad to you up to now. Hopefully things will be different from now on."

Connor rose from the table and gave his Dad a hug. Neither of them could remember the last time that had happened.

***

After school, Danny and Connor set out for the cove. The sea was half-way up the beach. Neither of them felt like swimming so sat on the steps waiting. Connor had retrieved the cloak from the cave and sat stroking the soft fur and gazing out to sea.

He sighed. "It's been an amazing few weeks! Everything has changed. What do you want to do Danny, when you leave school?"

"I'm definitely going to take Business Studies. I want to find out how you can set up your own business. I'd like a chain of grocery stores right across the islands. Do you think it would work?"

"I don't see why not. You've always been practical with a good business brain." He was gazing out to sea. "Look out Morag's coming and she's not alone."

Several figures were emerging from the water. A tall man with long white hair that was startlingly bright against his dark skin, a shorter woman with silvery hair that flowed down her back and around her shoulders, and Morag, holding hands with her little sister who had short black, curly hair, forming a dark halo around her head. Two other attendants stood behind the little group.

The boys walked slowly towards them, Connor holding

185

out the folded Selkie cloak. Connor had the urge to bow before this stately figure, but felt stupid at the thought, so just ducked his head slightly.

The woman took the cloak from Connor and handed it to one of the attendants.

"We are here to thank you for what you did for us." The man's voice rumbled like stones being rolled together by the tide. "We have brought gifts." The other attendant came forward and gave each of the boys a large exquisite fan-shaped shell just like the white mark on Shelly's Selkie cloak. One was decorated inside with blue and turquoise abalone, the other with the iridescent colours of mother-of-pearl.

Connor stepped forwards wondering why Morag was not her usual lively self.

"Thank you for these gifts. We're were glad to help. Morag is a great friend and I hope we can all become friends now."

"That is not possible," the tall man declared. "There can never be friendship between the Selkie and Men. Morag's disobedience was very fortunate for us, but the friendship has to come to an end." Connor's mouth fell open in disbelief. He looked towards Morag, taking in her stricken face.

"But..."

Morag's father raised his hand to silence Connor.

"We are moving away from these bitter waters and will not be seen here ever again. You may say your goodbyes now Morag!"

Morag moved stiffly towards the boys, she hugged Danny briefly whispering to him, then turned to Connor and clung to him as if she would never let him go, tears streaming from her eyes. He held onto her in turn biting his lip to stop his tears from flowing.

"You set me free Morag, I'll never forget you," his voice sounding rusty with unshed tears. Morag released him, wiping her face with the palm of her hand.

"Remember what I told you."

"Time to go," the rumbling voice declared.

Morag stumbled into the waves following her parents and didn't look back.

Connor pressed his fingers to his lips and closed his eyes willing the tears away. Danny threw an arm around his shoulders, holding him tight.

"You really liked her didn't you? I thought this might happen. I'm sorry Connor."

Connor pulled away. "It's alright. It was silly of me to think we could continue to be friends."

"You've still got me pal!"

Connor sighed, "Yeah, and you've still got me. What did she say to you Danny?"

"Food is my fortune. I guess I am going to make a success of the shop after all."

They walked up the beach together, the sinking sun lengthening their shadows and lighting up the cliff face, turning it gold.

END

EPILOGUE

Eight years later:

Hi Danny,
Thought it was time we had a catch-up. How's the shop going? I heard that you had opened another one. Hope it's going well.

I thought you'd like to know that my first solo exhibition is opening in a London gallery in two days' time. I'm flying down tomorrow. Thomas and Sasha will meet me there.

I'm going to try to come to the island and stay for a week or two at Mum and Dad's new house. Mum writes often. She's thrilled with all the mod cons. I'm surprised that Dad is still ferrying tourists around the islands although Mum says it's time he retired. Thank you for keeping an eye on them for me.

Life gets very busy sometimes and I long for the peace of the island. I'm glad Thomas and Sasha still have the Big House and that wonderful garden. They've got the right idea. A place of escape.

We haven't spent much time together since my operation. It's a shame we never got to play football after all. Maybe when I come we can have a game?

I think often of that crazy Summer holiday, of you and Morag, especially Morag, and wonder where she is now and is she safe.

Hope to see you in about three weeks' time.
All the best pal, and love to your lovely wife Fiona.

Connor

ABOUT THE AUTHOR

Barbara Evans was born in a small seaside town in south Wales, which features, with occasional adjustments, in some of her stories. She completed 'A' level Art at Swansea College of Art, then moved to Cheltenham and spent her time, when not working, among the art students and hippie poets of the town. She played guitar and sang Folk songs at the random gatherings held in her flat.

On moving to Rochester she developed a passion for traditional English folk songs, and performed in various Folk clubs. Some of these songs have been the inspiration for her stories.

She became an English teacher, married and raised a family who have now grown up and left home. So she has returned to her love of story writing where she enjoys travelling in the company of her characters and escaping into the lands and places her stories and poems create.

Printed in Great Britain
by Amazon